T0113331

Spider's Web

A Crash Site Story

Carter Johnson

authorHOUSE®

AuthorHouse™
1663 Liberty Drive
Bloomington, IN 47403
www.authorhouse.com
Phone: 1 (800) 839-8640

This is a work of fiction. All of the characters, names, incidents,
organizations, and dialogue in this novel are either the products
of the author's imagination or are used fictitiously.

Published by AuthorHouse 04/08/2016

ISBN: 978-1-5246-0114-0 (sc)
ISBN: 978-1-5246-0115-7 (e)

For my Dad,
who loves new worlds

November 7, 2027
6:17:42 PM
Impact minus 28 days

THE STREETS OF New Brooklyn were unusually quiet for this time of day. On a normal evening at this time, the streets would be filled with cars of every make and model, all jostling for position on the road. Normally, the traffic would be so heavy that running through it would be easy. Normally, the pedestrians were thick along the sidewalks, most of them wearing masks to cover their mouths and noses from the air pollution.

But today wasn't a normal day.

Victor Trace learned that very quickly as he ran up Avenue J, heading for Flatbush Avenue. After the mil-riots, Flatbush had been rebuilt as "affordable housing". It was the perfect place for Trace's operation. But now it was all going to hell. And when he made it back to his place, it would all go up in flames. Literally.

He looked over his right shoulder and caught a glimpse of the pale man in the black suit, now twenty yards or so behind him. The lack of traffic on the street was making it easier for him to move, but it did the same thing for the man in the black suit. Trace knew who the man was; or at least, who he worked for. The suit and the pale skin were dead giveaways. Another look over his shoulder told him that the man in the black suit had been joined by two other men wearing similar suits and just as pale.

Trace focused on the road ahead of him, crossing an intersection. He ignored the single car horn and kept moving. If he managed to get out of this alive and mobile, it would be the last glimpse he'd see of these streets for a very long time.

He could hear shouting behind him; the men in suits talking to each other. He couldn't make out the words, though. They were jumbled sounds to his ears. But he knew what they were talking about. Since he wasn't dead already, there was only one explanation: they wanted him alive. He could think of two reasons for that. He hoped they only knew about the one.

Flatbush opened up ahead of him, and Trace put on a burst of speed as he turned right. He could see the Thai restaurant which occupied the first floor of his building, and he could smell the scents of the food as it drifted from the open front door. Trace chanced another look behind him as he approached the restaurant.

Two of the pale men in suits where rounding the corner about twenty yards behind him. If he could make it to the building and get up the stairs, he had a reasonable chance of escape. He could take care of his files and equipment, then bolt for the roof and climb down the fire escape on the rear of the building. But he had to make it there first.

He nearly collided with a woman in an overcoat carrying paper grocery sacks in both hands, but he avoided the collision and spun around her on the left, continuing down the street. He was now only fifteen feet from the door which would take him up the stairs to his place. A final glance over his shoulder told him that the two men had now become four.

Trace pushed himself until he reached the door, then flung it open and yanked it shut. He threw the first and second bolts, then gave up and began his climb to the seventh floor. He passed his landlord, Mrs. Grable, in the stairway. "Get out," he told her, and he was on his way up the stairs once more.

At the seventh floor landing, Trace leapt over the railing and ran down the hallway towards his apartment. He could hear shouts coming from the tiny entryway below him; Mrs. Grable was being accosted as she tried to leave, more than likely. Trace ignored it and jammed his key into the lock, fumbling it. He cursed at himself, then tried again.

The door swung open and Trace threw himself into the darkened apartment. He slammed the door behind him and went down the door with his hand, flipping every lock into place. Then he lifted a sledgehammer from its place beside the front door and moved into the apartment, holding it on his right shoulder.

Computer terminals and servers of all makes and models filled the apartment. Cables and wires snaked across the floor, running every which way and disappearing into the apartment's walls. Trace moved towards the equipment and hefted the sledgehammer in both hands. He'd known this day would come eventually; it was, in its own way, a hazard of his job. It had only been a matter of time, and he had known that. But when he woke up this morning, the last thing he thought he'd be doing was this.

Trace raised the sledgehammer and brought it down on the first terminal. The computer shattered, sending sparks and slivers of plastic into the air. Trace gave it three more good whacks, then moved on. Each computer or server that he encountered was treated the same way. Sparks flew, and an acrid odor swirled through the air. He raised the sledgehammer and destroyed another terminal.

By the time he had finished with his task, he knew it was hopeless. There was no way out. He had spent too much time trying to sterilize his apartment and destroy any records he had left. He was only one man; the safety of the operation had to take priority over everything else. Otherwise, it would be gone overnight. He knew this in his head, but every instinct in his body was telling him to drop the sledgehammer and get the hell out.

The first blow crashed against his door with a resounding boom. *Too late.*

Trace ducked out of the main room and into the tiny space that served as his bedroom. Here, he flung his pillows off the tiny bed and reached for the SH15 pulse-pistol hidden beneath them. He checked the weapon to make sure it was loaded, then fled the room. This was it, he told himself. If he couldn't make it out of here, the least he could do was take some of them with him. They'd have no choice but to shoot him. He wouldn't have to worry about giving anything up, because he would be dead. And the operation would be secure for another day. It would just have to move along without him.

The blows to the door continued as Trace got into position, just a few feet away. When the door opened, he'd at least get the first two. The others would take him out, but it wouldn't matter. Everything was smashed. He'd reduced his computers and servers to scrap metal. They could try to retrieve the data, but it would be pointless.

The door crashed open a few moments later, slamming against the wall behind it and cracking the cheap plaster. Trace fired a burst from the pulse-pistol, hitting the first suited man in the chest. The man dropped, and another suited man stepped over his body as he came into the apartment. Trace and the man fired at the same time; only the suited man's rounds found their home. Trace's shots impacted the wall around the door, blowing small chunks of plaster into the air.

Trace dropped to the floor as a round blew out his left kneecap. Intense pain flooded his brain as he slumped to the hardwood floor. A second round to his right shoulder dropped the pulse-pistol from his hand as he tried to raise it once more. A third round put a neat hole in his left shoulder. He saw blackness closing in on all sides, creeping into his vision. It began to blot out everything …

Then he felt a hard slap across the left side of his face, and he was instantly brought back to a state of semi-consciousness. He could see a man kneeling in front of him as he felt his body begin to drop to the floor. Before it could, another suited man had grabbed his shoulders, holding him up. The first suited man, the one kneeling in front of him, holstered his own weapon and glared at Trace. "You know why we are here, Mr. Trace," said the suited man.

Trace found the words easily enough, but he stumbled on them as he spoke. "Fuck you, MIB. Finish me off because I'm not gonna tell you shit."

The suited man smiled. "Oh, but you will, Mr. Trace. You see, we know what it is that you do here. We know about your network."

Trace knew this was a lie. If they had the network, they wouldn't be talking to him like this. They would've put a bullet in his head as soon as they came through the door. "Bullshit," he managed. "You've got nothing. That's why you're here."

"Regardless," the suited man said, his pale skin reflecting the late evening sunset. "We know that you are part of this network. We know what you do here."

Trace kept his face blank. He wouldn't give them anything. "Shoot me already."

The suited man shook his head. "No. You will tell us what we want to know."

Trace raised one hand to the man's face; the suited man backed off an inch or two, but stopped when he saw that Trace's hand was empty. Trace lifted one finger and drew it across the suited man's cheek, smearing the white makeup. Beneath it, Trace could see pinkish skin with a slight growth of stubble. He managed a smile. "So you assholes aren't mandroids, huh? Just flesh and bone, like me."

The suited man pushed Trace's hand down to the floor, keeping that same smile on his face. "Stay on topic, Mr. Trace. Give us what we want and we will spare you. There is a hospital only twelve blocks from here. We can get you there in time to save your life."

Another lie; Trace knew he was going to die on this floor in his shitty apartment. There was nothing he could do about it now. Things had gone to shit far too quickly. He was done for. "You expect me to believe that, MIB?"

The suited man turned to one of his comrades and held out his hand. "Give it to me."

The second suited man removed a wicked-looking piece of shiny metal from within his jacket and handed it to the first man. The object was cylindrical, with a hooked barb on one end. The first suited man turned the device over in his hand, then held it out for Trace to see. "Do you know what this is?" the suited man asked. When Trace did not answer, he continued. "It is an extractor. You see, I simply jam this into your shoulder like so—" The suited man bent down and shoved the device into one of Trace's new holes. A surge of pain filled his body and he fought down the urge to scream. "—and it removes the bullets for me. A rather effective form of torture, don't you think? And if I run out, I can simply put more into you until you die." He withdrew the device; the hooked barb on the end now held a small flattened bullet. The suited man pressed a small button on the device's stalk and the bullet dropped to the floor. He held the device up once more. "Shall we continue?"

Trace weighed it in his mind. If he gave up the operation, everything would be lost. The entire network would collapse overnight, dismantled by men just like the one kneeling in front of him. Hundreds of people would be killed, and many more would disappear into ghost prisons. The network had to be protected, at all costs. He had no problem giving up his own life for it. He had known that was a risk when he joined the operation. But to be responsible for its downfall? That was not something he wanted on his conscience, no matter how little time he had left. On the other hand, if he gave up the girl … It had to be done, he told himself. Her life was worth the safety of the network. She was only one girl.

"Stop," Trace finally said. "Please. I'll tell you."

The suited man backed off, getting to his feet. He returned the device to the second suited man and said, "Excellent. Everything, please, from top to bottom."

Trace shook his head. "I don't know that." He hoped the look on his face conveyed pain and truth. He couldn't afford to leave any suspicions. "It's compartmentalized. We only know our own part."

"And? What was yours?"

Trace tried to look conflicted, hoping it would help to sell his story. "I move them down the line to their Surgeons. I set up the appointments. That's it."

"You're not lying to me, are you?"

Trace shook his head once more. "That's all I know."

The suited man bent at the waist, putting his face only inches from Trace's own. "That's not enough, Mr. Trace. I'm afraid that I'll need more than that."

Trace dropped his eyes, staring at the floor. He told himself once again that her life was worth it. She was only one girl. "Jennifer. That's all I know. She didn't give me a last name. She didn't say anything else. All I know is where she's going."

"And where is that?"

"The Red District in Millennium City. Dusseldorf Avenue. Her Surgeon operates out of a back-alley medical facility there. She's going to be there tomorrow night."

"I need a time."

"I don't have one. I just make the calls."

The suited man stood up and was silent for several moments. Then he turned to his colleague. "Tear this place apart. I'll call it in." Then he turned his gaze back to Trace. "Is that everything?"

Trace nodded. "I swear, I don't know anything else." He hoped the man believed him.

"Good. Now, I bid you *adieu*, Mr. Trace. If there is an afterlife, of which I am dubious, please try to enjoy it." He drew his weapon and began to aim.

Trace found he had a smile on his face as he faced his own death. There was a strange sense of calm that swept over him, as if he had been ready for this moment his entire life. He figured in some way, he probably was. There was nothing left to say, no moves left to make. This was it. And he found that he was okay with that.

~~~

The suited man pointed his weapon at Trace's head. "Goodbye, Mr. Trace." He fired twice, both rounds striking Victor Trace in the forehead and destroying the back of his skull. Brain matter and gore splattered the hardwood floor beneath Trace's now-lifeless body, creating a bloody canvass. The suited man examined the mess for a few seconds, then turned away.

He withdrew a smartphone from the inside pocket of his jacket and quickly dialed a number.

The phone rang twice, then a gruff voice answered. "Yes?"

The suited man instantly stood up a little straighter, and his eyes became bright. "Sir, this is Agent Ellis. We have completed the mission."

"Anything to report?"

"We have a location for tomorrow evening, sir. In Millennium City. Looks like an implant removal."

"Good. Every little piece, Ellis, every little piece. We're getting closer."

"Yes, sir."

The gruff voice cleared its throat, then said, "Is there any recoverable data?"

"Negative, sir. Looks like Trace destroyed everything he could before we broke the door down."

"Damn." There was a moment of silence, then the voice said, "Clean it up, Ellis. No traces. Get back here immediately. We have an operation to plan."

"Yes, sir." The suited man, Agent Ellis, hung up the phone and slipped it back into his jacket. Then he turned to the man standing next to him, Agent Holland, and said, "Check the kitchen for a gas line. These piece of shit places should still have them. Yank it and let's get out of here."

"Yes, sir," said Agent Holland, and the man disappeared into the apartment's tiny kitchen.

Agent Ellis holstered his weapon and turned away from the body. He had a sneaking suspicion that Trace hadn't told them everything. There was no way for him to quantify this feeling, but he had always trusted his instincts. And right now, something was telling him that this wasn't all of it. Some part of his mind knew that Trace had withheld certain things. Maybe he knew more about the internal leadership of the operation than he had let on. If so, they had just squandered a valuable resource. But then again, he had orders, and those orders did not involve letting Victor Trace live.

Agent Holland returned from the kitchen. "It's done."

"Good." Ellis turned towards the door, where a third man named Agent Graves was standing guard. Not that they would have many problems here. This building, and the neighborhood it stood in, was filled with people who just wanted to get through the day. They had no desire to get involved in other people's problems. In short, they would mind their own business.

The two agents exited the apartment while Agent Graves took up the rear. It wouldn't take long for the gas to find an ignition source, not in a building like this. He knew that this part of New Brooklyn had been rebuilt by the lowest bidder using the cheapest materials possible. Nothing would remain once the gas caught.

The three agents exited the apartment building and walked casually down the street. No one noticed them, or paid any attention if they did. The three pale men in black suits passed through the neighborhood without incident and disappeared into the approaching darkness.

2

November 8, 2027
9:52:17 PM
Impact minus 27 days

THE 2019 HALPERIN Farmiga pulled off of Desperation Avenue and into the Vertical Automobile Storage Unit, leaving behind a nasty rainstorm. The Farmiga's 5.8 liter V-8 rumbled beneath the hood, while the stereo system shook the car's frame. It drove through the bomb scanners without incident, due in part to a lack of maintenance on the detectors themselves. Although there was no bomb on board the car, the scanners wouldn't have picked it up anyway. The machinery was aging, and management seemed to be letting it happen. But what else was new around here?

The Farmiga drove through a large open area and onto the ascending platform. The engine switched off and the door opened, disgorging the driver.

Spider

Spider wore his best black pinstriped Idio Nagata suit
tonight, paired with a fluorescent orange Boyega tie. His
peroxide-white hair stuck out in every direction, vaguely
resembling an anime villain. He closed the Farmiga's door
and stepped off the platform, crossing the open area to a
plastiglass booth several yards away. He could hear gears
grinding behind him as the platform rose, his Farmiga
going with it. His eyes tried to avoid the neon billboards
and framed advertisements that assaulted him on the
way, but it was no use. Hula Girl Gin, Farmer's Vodka,
Kaneda Premium Cigarettes, Detox Cola, Tatsu Green
Tea; he saw them all.

The Service Bot wired up inside the booth turned towards him as he approached, its servo-motors whirring beneath it. Spider reached into the left pocket of his pants and pulled out a small credit card-like slip of plastic. The Service Bot switched on its artificial smile. "Good evening, citizen. Welcome to the Prospect Parking Corporation's Vertical Automobile Storage Unit. How can Service Bot designate George help you today?"

"Park it, screw-head," Spider growled. He was already in a bad mood because of the heavy traffic getting out of Yellow District. He swiped the plastic card through a reader mounted outside the booth.

The Service Bot was silent for a moment, then it said, "Thank you, Phillip Huxley." The artificial smile became a frown. "Service Bot George must inform you that you have not paid your fees in—" It searched its database. "Four months. Please swipe your credit-slash-debit card below, or use the palm-scanner to pay with an implant."

Spider shook his head, debating. If he didn't pay the fees, he'd never get the Farmiga back again. These VASUs were designed to deter thieves, and consequently, they were built to be impassable to anything besides Service Bots (and rats, because they could never be kept out). He could try to break the car out, but it would be nearly impossible. And more trouble than it was worth. He swore under his breath and said, "Pay with card." He didn't like the idea of implanting a payment device under his skin. Besides, that would mean using his own money. He took out a second card and swiped it.

The Service Bot switched on its smile once more. "Thank you, Phillip Huxley." The Bot took a few moments to process the payment, then it said, "Your fees have been paid."

"You and my toaster would make a great couple," Spider muttered.

A blue ticket was spat from a machine beneath the palm-scanner, and Spider snatched it away. He pocketed the ticket inside his jacket, then began to turn away.

The Service Bot said, "Have a nice day."

Spider found he couldn't resist. "Go stick your finger in a light socket." He laughed as he crossed the open area once more. He made his way to a small steel door set into the VASU's concrete structure. The door was closed, keeping the city air and the riff-raff out, but Spider knew they were there, just on the other side of the door. The Red awaited him, as it did nearly every night. Before he could push the door open, he caught sight of a glowing neon frame just a few feet from the door. Inside the frame was a poster of a young Japanese girl, no older than twenty, holding a microphone in one hand and cupping her right breast with the other. Spider shook his head. Yumi was everywhere now. The Japanese pop singer's face and songs were unavoidable, especially here. He caught a glimpse of the writing along the bottom: *Catch Yumi Tonight Live at Dragon's Tears! One Night Only!* At least he knew which section of the Red to avoid this evening.

Spider pushed the door open and walked out of the VASU into an oily rainstorm, dodging two vacant-eyed info-junkies as his feet found the sidewalk without his knowledge. His mind was focused on the night's business, after which he could relax for a few hours until something else came up. He tossed both his parking card and the credit card he had used to pay the fees onto the street, not giving either a second look. Since they were both stolen, it didn't matter.

The rain slid down his neck, leaving slick traces of pollution against his skin. The air quality was improving with the rain, at least. A man dressed in a black coverall with spikes protruding from both shoulders removed the gas mask from his face, taking a breath of fresh air. The man smiled as the rain splashed against his skin.

Spider ran a hand through his hair as he stepped off the sidewalk and into the street. A group of Harajuku Girls stood, laughing and giggling, on the other side of Desperation Avenue, all purple hair and green furry boots and neon eyes. Spider avoided colliding with one, who shouted at him in Mandarin that he should watch his step. He casually flipped her the finger and continued on his way.

The Red was jumping tonight, he thought, more so than usual. He could see only one prostitute lounging against the glass front of Eddie's Sushi Bar and Noodle House. The girl, no older than twelve, stood in a puddle of neon casually smoking an off-brand Chinese cigarette. Her friends, the same girls Spider saw every night, were busy talking with several Russian businessmen in hushed tones. On a normal night, the three girls would all be leaning against the glass, shouting lewd phrases to passersby in the hope of getting a date. But tonight, it seemed, the girls were doing brisk business. He caught a few sentences as he passed behind the girls, whispered phrases of Russian that mostly translated to, "That costs extra."

Spider found he had a smile on his face at the hookers' words. Everything was extra here in the Red, no matter what.

He waited for a group of giggling teenage Jahdanka Girls to pass by on his left, no doubt heading for the Yumi concert. He mused for just a moment on the fact that the Red could assimilate nearly any cultural or fashion trends. Take the Jahdanka Girls, for example. They were nothing more than an Americanized version of the Harajuku Girls he had seen down the street, named after a particular neighborhood inside the Red District. The only difference? Jahdanka Girls were American, whereas Harajuku Girls were Japanese. Or take Yumi herself. The Red fetishized her like no other place on the planet. Even in her home country of Japan, she wasn't worshipped the way she was here. If the Red District had a deity, it would be her. Then he let the thoughts pass as he ducked into the small door to his right.

Doom's Market was not the friendliest place to do your grocery shopping. The clientele were somewhat distasteful, according to Spider's personal preferences. But then again, he had been told that his preferences were not normal. The place itself lacked proper air-conditioning in the summer and heat in the winter. Just like now. Spider felt the Red's polluted air follow him inside.

The smell of fried meats and stale cigarettes assaulted his nose as down-tempo synth-pop filled his ears. Beneath the usual smells, he could detect a hint of marijuana, probably from Doom himself, along with spices that he could not place and the scent of freshly brewed coffee. He could see a line of customers near the counter; Future Goths, cyberpunks, circuiters, junkies. Everyone that lived in this part of town shopped here.

Doom was behind the counter, wearing his usual X-Specs and D-Note personal music device. He gave Spider a cursory glance and a chin jut of recognition, then went back to the line of customers in front of his register. Cigarettes, beer, liquor, shaving cream, and toilet paper: those were the things Doom specialized in. His reasoning? Everybody needed those things constantly. You could pick up fresh produce and other food items, to be sure, but these were the staples of Doom's Market.

Spider walked through the market until he found the back of the line. He was eleven people away from the register.

He waited as patiently as he could, checking his phone for messages and using it to scroll through his news sites for any tidbits. When he was five people away, he slid the phone back into his jacket. Finally, he made it.

Doom gave him a casual scowl and asked, "What do you want, Spider?"

"I need some smokes, Doom."

The grubby man turned around and began to reach for a pack of Russian knockoffs from the full shelf behind him.

"Not that shit, Doom. The good stuff. American."

"Got nothing for you, Spider." Doom turned around to face him.

"Come on, man. I just need the one pack for now."

"I told you, I've got nothing. Move it along."

Spider reached into his jacket and withdrew a wad of bills. "I'll give you thirty for it."

"Fine." Doom reached beneath the counter and pulled out a pack of Addison Premiums, slapping it down. "Money."

Spider slid two bills across the counter. "You're a true humanitarian, Doom, you know that? A real nice guy."

"Fuck yourself, Spider. Move it along."

Laughing, Spider tucked the pack of cigarettes into his jacket and left the market.

Back on the street, Spider turned left out of the market and continued up Desperation Avenue. The blue backlit sign attached to the light post ahead caught his eye: Lexington Street. Here, he knew, was the invisible demarcation line that signaled the end of Haitian territory and the beginning of Triad turf. Neither gang operated much on Desperation Avenue. That was strictly for business like separating tourists from their money, dealing out the back door, and selling skin. But if he were to turn right and travel down Lexington Street, he would find the Haitians patrolling their land. And he would be stopped, just like everyone else. They would leave him alone, once they discovered who he was, but others wouldn't be so lucky.

He stepped to his left as he crossed Lexington and let a group of Future Goths pass by, taking in their black leather and chrome spikes and illegal Electronic Body Modifications. His eye fixed on a woman with dark pink hair, who had a Glass Eye implant connected to a removable headset that he had never seen. He caught the make and model number on the back of the headset as the girl passed by him, and he made a mental note to check it with Thrash when he got back to the club.

The rain picked up before Spider could move, so he backed up several paces until he was covered by the overhang of a large apartment building. He could smell noodles and fish coming from the restaurant on the ground floor, and he was tempted to step inside for a few minutes. Grab a bite to eat and maybe get out of the rain. But he dismissed the notion. He could always send Severen for takeout when he got back. Spider lit a cigarette instead, reveling in the taste of the American tobacco. He took a long drag and blew smoke into the rain, watching it dissipate. A few seconds later, the rain let up enough that he knew he could make it. He took a final drag of the cigarette and pitched it away. He had things to do.

Ahead, he could see two drunken Canadians stumbling out of a bath house, still wearing their towels, as a small Japanese woman shouted at them from the bath house's front door. Several articles of clothing followed the woman's words into the street, instantly soaked by the polluted rain. The Canadians, laughing hysterically, gathered their soiled garments and took off running down Desperation Avenue.

Spider was chuckling to himself at the Canadians as he passed the mouth of the alley, and consequently, he wasn't looking. The two thugs, both dressed in camouflage and wearing the insignia and colors that identified them as Chinese Triad, were on Spider before he could react. They dragged him deep into the alley and flung him to its disgusting ground. Spider felt himself sink into a heap of rotting garbage. His only thought was the Rolex on his right wrist, and how long it would take to get the smell off.

The two thugs were now standing a few feet away from him. Both were brandishing pulse-pistols aimed at his head. In the darkness of the alley, it was difficult to make out their features, but Spider got a good look. And when he did, he began to laugh. The sound echoed up and down the alleyway, sending a stray cat diving for cover behind a Dumpster. His laugh caught the two Triad thugs off-guard. They had been expecting him to beg for his life, he knew. And now? *This is going to be good*, he thought. *Real good*.

"Which one of you fucking idiots wants to call your boss and show him my face?" Spider asked. He dug into his pocket and held out his smartphone to the two men. "Go ahead. Use my phone. Turn the camera on too, so he can get a good look at me."

The thug nearest to the alley's exit now dropped his mouth open. For several seconds, he simply stared at Spider like this. "Well?" Spider asked. "Who wants to make the call? Which one of you morons is gonna be tomorrow's cold fish?" He shook his head, chuckling now, and picked himself up. The garbage smell had already infiltrated his suit, he knew, and it would never come out. Millennium City garbage had a way of sticking around for a long time afterwards, like a bad dose of the clap. Spider shook his head again, now angry about his suit, and turned his eye to the two thugs. "And give me your names. Whichever one of you is still alive is gonna pay for the dry-cleaning on this suit. This is an Idio Nagata original, you fucking assholes." He shook the phone in his hand. "So make the call already. Let's get this over with."

The first thug finally closed his mouth, swallowed, then asked, "Who the hell are you anyway?"

"Some mouthy asshole," said the second thug. "Now hand over your shit before we have to get rough." He waved the pulse-pistol in his hand.

Spider laughed again. "Please do. That'll make it all the sweeter when you finally make the call. Please."

"Who are you?" asked the first thug, his voice firmer now. "And don't crack wise again."

"I'm Spider. I do a lot of … business with your boss. And his boss. And his boss's boss. So if I were you, I'd turn around and quietly walk away before I make the call myself."

"Shit," said the first thug. "Shit on me."

"Not if you leave now, I won't," said Spider. "Now go."

The two thugs shared a look that lasted a few seconds, then they turned away from Spider and left the alley, blending into the crowds on the street.

Spider pocketed his phone and brushed the front of his suit off, cursing silently. He wasn't kidding about the cleaning bill. And he knew just where to send it.

Back on the street, Spider decided it would be best to run his errand now and get back to the club before he ran into any more trouble. Not everyone on the street was as understanding as the Triads. At least they knew how to do business. The Arabs and the Jews would kill you over a bad look in the street or over dinner. Over the years, he had learned that every group he did business with had its own code, its own way about it. Prudence dictated that he learn the subtle differences, or it would cost him more than a blown deal.

Drag queens spilled out of the bar to his left, suddenly enveloping him. He could smell exotic perfumes and hair products; he could see lace and satin and fake nails. Then they were gone into the street, cackling and crowing about something or other. Spider paid little attention as he moved on.

He stopped at the next intersection, waiting with the crowd for the light to change. His little encounter had put an extra ounce of caution into his step, and he was dubious of crossing in late-night traffic. Something like sixty-four pedestrians were hit every day in the Red, and of those sixty-four, twenty-one were killed. He didn't want to be a statistic. He blended into the group as best he could. Now that his suit smelled like trash, he had no doubt that the Red would accept him as one of its own. He received no strange looks from the Harajuku Girls, who had migrated down the street during his encounter with the Triad thugs; or from the Orthodox Christians gathered tightly together against the sin around them; or from the info-junkies who busied themselves with learning everything they could in the span of a few seconds. Spider found he was just like everyone else tonight, and he didn't like it.

The light changed and Spider crossed the street with the group. He found his eyes roaming the motley collection of people before him. There was a couple dressed in future wear holding hands in front of a sushi bar, bathed in neon. Crossing the street to his left were a group of blond American teenagers dressed like Japanese schoolgirls, their eyes glassy from the opium den where they had no doubt been peddling themselves. On the corner ahead of him was a strip club that specialized in custom fantasies and advertised *No Taboos* with a red neon sign clipped to the front window. He could see a dark-haired fourteen year old girl just getting off her shift as she left the club, a black Russian cigarette clamped between her teeth. She bumped into his shoulder as she hurried past him across the street, and he could barely hear her muttered, "Sorry, mister" as she continued on. How did he know her age? The eyes. It was always the eyes. When the body and the face were that young, and the eyes were that old, fourteen was her age. At least it was here in the Red. He wondered how the other city districts were faring these days, but just like everyone else in the Red, he only really cared about Blue District. That was where life was nice as pie and twice as sweet. Clean air, no crime, and nothing but sunshine to waste your days in. Sounded like the life to him.

Spider walked another two blocks through the crowds and the taxis and the hookers and the rain before he spotted the glow of that familiar neon sign. He smiled, ready to be shed of the wad of cash stuffed into his jacket. Walking around here with it was just asking for trouble, but he knew he'd never find parking anywhere near Mother's place. He'd be damned if he was going to leave a slick ride like his Farmiga just sitting on the street in the middle of the Red. That was not good business.

Mother's place, called Dark Desires, was just like any other sex shop in the Red. He could hear sleazy dance music pumping inside the store as he approached the door. The front windows were filled with the Kobiyashi Robotics Corporation's newest Eroto-Bots, the Gen 3. Spider could see the blond model, Sophie the Sexpot, standing front and center with one hand on a jutting hip. She was flanked by the other models of her generation, Andi Does Anal and Brianna the Bedhopper. The Bots were dressed in revealing outfits made of vinyl, and each one wore a sign around her neck that read *Only $4999.95! Ask About Our Special Financing Deals!* Propped up below them was a piece of cardboard with a crude computer-printed sign on it that read *Understands and Responds to over 2,000 voice commands! Available in English, Spanish, Japanese, Chinese, and German language editions! Now available with 8 different hair colors!* Spider shook his head as he pushed the front door open and cringed when a bell above his head rang out his entrance. He'd never liked those damn bells.

Inside, his eyes took in the shop: Kobiyashi Corporation's licensed Bot-Wear clothing filled the first few aisles, along with boxes of shoes in every size and color. Spider moved past this display into the store proper, where he was suddenly surrounded by sex toys of all sizes. Glass massagers and plastic dildos seemed to glare at him from the shelves. He turned in a circle to get his bearings, then found himself staring at a plastiglass booth tucked into one corner of the store. Behind the plastiglass was a balding fat man with dirt under his nails and a tattoo of a dancing girl snaking down his neck and under his grimy shirt collar.

Mother

"Mother," Spider began as he crossed the shop to the booth, "you look like I feel right now."

The balding man looked up from his tablet computer, and now Spider could see the illegal corneal implants in Mother's eyes. He pointed to them as he reached the booth. "Nice EBM, Mother. When did you get those?"

"Six nights ago," the balding man replied, his voice like the crunch of gravel under tires. "Found a Surgeon off of Beal Street that did it for two grand and some store credit." He blinked, and Spider could see the unnatural blue light that now surrounded the balding man's corneas. "No more glasses, and I can get rid of the door-scanners in another week or so. Don't need 'em now. I can tell instantly if somebody's got jazz up their sleeve or not."

Spider reached into his jacket and withdrew a plain white envelope stuffed with cash. He plopped it down on the counter and slid it through a 4-inch slit in the plastiglass. "This week's cut, as promised."

Mother reached for the envelope, then stopped. His pug nose inhaled the air around him, then he grimaced and cocked an eyebrow at Spider. "Is that you?"

Spider nodded. "Unfortunately, yes."

"What the fuck happened?" Then he grinned. "I told you to stay away from those girls on Catholic Street. That road is aptly named." He tucked the envelope beneath the counter without glancing at it.

"Thanks for the advice. And no, that isn't what happened. Had a run-in with two Triad boys on the way over here. Knocked me into a pile of garbage in some piece of shit alley. They didn't know who they were fucking with."

Mother's grin remained. "Did you play nice with them?"

"More or less. Their pride might be a little hurt, but that's all. For now. And they owe me for this suit. It's an Idio Nagata."

"Sure, sure. Hey, Quartez called here about five minutes ago to see if you'd been in yet. Says there's a job waiting for you back at the club. Told me to tell you to call in when you got here."

"I'll wait, thanks." A job could mean anything, and he wasn't in that big of a hurry, now that the cash was off him. He'd get back to the club when he got back. His earlier cautiousness was quickly forgotten as he thought about the bar only two blocks further down Desperation Avenue, a place called The Covenant. There was one girl in particular ...

"So now that you're here," Mother began, ignorant of Spider's internal reverie, "can I interest you in a new Bot? I got the latest Gens here, and all the accessories you could ever need."

Spider turned away from the counter, heading into the store, and called out over his shoulder, "Still prefer the real thing, Mother. Take it easy."

"Hey, watch your back out there," Mother shouted to him. "It's a jungle, you know?"

"No shit," Spider muttered, as he opened the front door and left the store.

On the street, he blended in behind a group of German sex tourists, here because of the Red's reputation. Digital cameras and smartphones clicked away at nearly everything in sight. Spider wove his way around the group and sped up his pace to keep them behind him as he reached another intersection. Here, traffic was slower. The human cab drivers screamed at their Bot counterparts in JR Cab Corporation taxis on his right, while pedestrians streamed past him on the left. A young Japanese girl, dressed in form-fitting pink latex and carrying a clear plastic umbrella brushed past him, and Spider nearly broke her arm as he snatched his wallet out of her hand. The girl disappeared into the crowd, cradling her arm, before he could do or say anything else. The encounter lasted two or three seconds; Spider wondered how many times she had pulled it tonight. He shook his head and kept on.

The intersection of Desperation Avenue and Kilgore Street was a popular hang-out for the hookers and the info-junkies, due in large part to the news screens sunk high into the buildings around them. The info-junkies could look away from their phones and tablets and illegal EBMs for just a few moments, and not lose their fix. The hookers could ply their trade on the so-called businesspeople that frequented the corner for their brief taste of news. Spider threw a smile to a young hooker he knew named Odessa, who was leaning against the driver's door of a late-model Halperin Ghost. She gave him a wink as he passed by, then turned back to the Japanese businessman behind the Ghost's wheel. Spider heard Odessa say, "That'll cost extra" in Japanese before he was out of earshot.

The rain had washed most of the garbage from his suit, but barring a miracle, it was more than likely ruined. Might as well put it to good use, he thought. As he crossed Kilgore Street to the other side, passing between a JR Cab and a brand-new Valmont Chassis, he looked up at one of the news screens to catch a glimpse. The bleach-blond behind the news desk was nearly inaudible in the din of the Red around him, but he could just read the scrolling text at the bottom of the screen. It looked as though the Triads had killed the Haitian gang leader, Papa Batuu, in a shootout only two hours before. The text told him that this had happened on the other side of the Red, so deep that the police wouldn't even go inside. Not that they came into the Red much anyway. The neighborhoods here were on their own, and they knew it. So they formed watch groups and took care of their own blocks. Spider had heard it called street justice, but he disagreed. When the cops wouldn't come into your neighborhood and do something about the problem, then it was up to you. Spider had grown up in what was left of Brooklyn after the millennium riots, and he knew that this was a truth most of the world did not like. It was a hard truth, and it was a brutal truth, but it was a truth nonetheless.

Spider turned away from the screens and dodged past another hooker he knew named Daniella, who tossed him a smile and a very coquettish "Hi, Spider" as he passed her. He made a note to revisit this corner tomorrow night, when he wasn't so busy. Before he could go further, the rain increased once more, and all around him, people dashed out of the streets to hide under the eaves of roofs and beneath canopies. He himself ducked beneath the Hotel Spedley's canopy, nodding to the doorman and admiring his chrome submachine gun. He lit another cigarette, intending to smoke this one whether the rain let up or not.

He was halfway through it when the rain did, in fact, let up.

Spider stood beneath the canopy for another minute or two until the cigarette was finished, then he deposited the butt unceremoniously on the street outside the Hotel Spedley. He joined a crowd of body-mod enthusiasts headed up the block towards the next intersection, the same direction Spider was headed. If he could get there in the next two minutes, he'd have time to catch a little of tonight's opening act while he had his drink.

The body-mod crowd ducked into a tattoo parlor halfway down the block, and Spider was once again a lone entity moving through a sea of other lone entities. Street hustlers did business outside of a computer repair shop, an obvious front for drug-dealing. Nobody in the

Red needed their computers fixed. When the machine broke, you got a new one. The people that didn't follow that philosophy had no need of repair services, since they could fix their own machines. Spider passed the hustlers without incident.

The Covenant was on the next corner, and he made it there with thirty seconds to spare. Spider pushed past a group of glassy-eyed info-junkies as he made his way into the bar, settling into an empty stool just as the emcee was finishing his spiel. Spider ordered up a gin and tonic from the Bot bartender, then turned his attention to the stage as the Bot set to work making his drink.

Music came up from hidden speakers. After the first few seconds, Spider recognized it as a cover of "Cities in Dust", redone with a dance beat. The song brought a smile to his face. At least some of these barbarians had good taste in music. Then, as he watched, three teenage girls came out from backstage, each dressed entirely in a different color; red, white, and blue. Spider recognized their outfits from a decade-old cartoon called *Stranger Danger*, but he wondered if anyone else in the audience made the connection. He doubted it.

The Bot served him his drink, and Spider sipped it as he watched the teenagers bounce and dance across the stage to the music, performing various lewd acts as they did to the delight of the crowd. Spider had become immune to such things over time. As usual, he chalked it up to a simple job hazard. When you worked out of a titty joint, you were bound to become used to it. He took another sip of his drink.

When the song was over, the three girls collected their outfits from the stage's floor and scrambled behind the closing curtain. The emcee came back out, dressed in a

CARTER JOHNSON

shiny gold suit and holding a microphone in one hand. Spider didn't stick around to listen. Instead, he finished his drink and tossed a ten onto the bar. He gathered himself up and walked out the door.

The rain had not quit, but it had let up a tad more since he had ducked into The Covenant. Spider looked at his watch; it was almost ten-forty. He wiped a speck of grime from the watch's face, then continued on down Desperation Avenue. He was four blocks from the club.

Those blocks passed in a blur of neon and nameless faces, the same things he saw every night in the Red. Some of the faces he recognized, but could not name. Some of them he knew, but avoided out of necessity. Others he avoided out of spite, and still others he dodged simply because they annoyed him. But everywhere around him were the people of the Red, and the tourists who came every night for cheap drinks and cheaper thrills.

3

THE CAT O' Nine Club was located on the corner of Desperation Avenue and Colton Street. In truth, it extended down Desperation nearly to the next intersection. The club was massive, with three stories of entertainment and all the pleasures you could imagine. You just had to know where to look, and who to ask. A red and green neon sign hung just above the club's entrance, depicting a whip lashing through the air. Spider swung the door open and stepped inside, glad to finally be out of the rain for the evening. He had no intention of leaving the club now. If he got hungry, he'd simply send Thrash or Severen for food when he made it to the Hive.

A blast of heated air, filled with the unmistakable smell of scented pheromones, hit him face first as he came inside, letting the door close itself behind him. A dance beat dripping with bass filled his ears. More of Quartez's influence. His eyes took a few moments to adjust to the dimness of the club's interior. When they did, he could make out the same Greeter-Bot, designated Faith, behind the same dark wood desk in the same corner of the lobby as when he had left three hours before. Before the Greeter-Bot could raise her carbon-fiber hand at him, Spider waved the Bot away and said, "Spider's back, nuts and bolts. Let Quartez know."

"Certainly, sexy," the Greeter-Bot responded in a robotic, but not unattractive, voice.

Spider pushed open the massive double doors that led into the club proper, and was once again hit in the face with scented pheromones and dance music. The club was filled with cigarette smoke, both genuine and imitation, which he had to wave away in order to see. On the stage, Janessa and Dauphine and Ellegarta were in the middle of their Snow White routine. Dauphine wore only a red corset and held a large red apple in one hand while Janessa, dressed as the Evil Queen, swatted at her with a leather flogger. Ellegarta danced behind them, dressed as what Spider thought was supposed to be Prince Charming, moving her hips in time to the music. Soon, the other girls would join them, dressed as the Seven Dwarves, to release their friend and defeat the Evil Queen. Not exactly Disney, Spider thought, but it was better than what he'd seen at The Covenant.

He moved through the club, his eyes roaming the new and familiar faces within the large crowd of people. He could see Texas Eddie in the corner with Bella and Aria, as he was nearly every night. And there, nearest to the stage, was Norkus Vile, the Red's one and only celebrity, who played guitar and sang vocals in a post-neo-punk band called Dorkus McVorkus. Vile was busy dividing his time between the stage show and the strippers who were grinding against him. Spider dodged around tables and chairs, avoiding the occasional "Hey, Spider". Across the club, he found the staircase and began the climb.

Second floor. Here, he found the main VIP area, as well as another bar. He abandoned the stairs and crossed the area to the bar, where he was met by an actual human being instead of a Bot. Bridgit was tending tonight, and the redhead met Spider with her usual thousand-watt smile as he slipped onto a stool. His eyes were drawn to the tattoo on her neck. A large gold band encircled it like a string of pearls. From here, it looked like a piece of jewelry, a choker necklace she could put on and take off at will. Spider knew the truth; it was actually a halo. If you saw the white angel wings tattooed on her back, the whole thing made sense. "Your usual, Spider?" Bridgit asked, her whiskey-and-cigarettes voice sending a chill up Spider's spine. She was already a redhead, Spider's kryptonite, but with that voice? She knew what she was doing. "Or do you want to try something else tonight?" She was laying it on thick now, and Spider found himself more than a little tempted. But he had business to do first.

Bridgit

So he shook his head and answered, "Just the usual tonight, Bridgit." Then he winked at her. "For now."

The bartender turned away from him to make his drink, and Spider looked out onto the club.

The ladies had finished their Snow White routine, and the stage had cleared for the moment. But Spider knew that Dauphine would be back out shortly to perform her fire-dance. That one he enjoyed, mostly for the danger, but he had other things to do tonight. When Bridgit handed him a glass full of extra dry gin and tonic, he took a long sip.

"What is that smell?" Bridgit asked, shouting over the music. "Is that you, Spider?"

He nodded. "I almost got mugged by some Triad goons on the way to Mother's. They tossed me into some garbage, and now my suit is ruined. It's an Idio Nagata."

"It was. Now it's cleaning rags."

"Time will tell." He sipped his drink. "You seen Quartez tonight?"

Bridgit shook her head. "Last time I saw her, she was on the third floor. That group from K-Corp is here again." She shuddered. "I hate those guys, Spider. They creep me out."

He grinned at her. "That's because they want to eat sushi off of you, and you can't stand raw fish."

"They only requested it once," Bridgit responded. "But that costs extra."

"So does everything around here." He downed the drink in two swallows, then set the glass on the bar. "You working all night?"

"Right here. Come find me later. Maybe I'll let you walk me home."

"Maybe I will." He stood up and tossed a twenty onto the bar. "For the drink."

"You know your money's no good here."

"Keep it anyway." Spider left the bar and headed for the stairs.

Spider knew, just as Bridgit did, that the third floor was the true VIP area. It was where Quartez catered to her most discerning clients, with the utmost discretion. Those were the words she liked to use, anyway. Spider knew Quartez was nothing more than a whorehouse madam, just as he knew that he was nothing more than a thief. But they both kept up appearances, for the sake of their reputations. Maybe that was why he was allowed to do business here, and to rent the space from her. As he topped the stairs, he could see the woman, bent low over a table surrounded by men in suits that made his look like cheap polyester. Quartez wore a white silk kimono with red and blue designs scrawled across it. Her thick brown hair was piled atop her head and held in place with chopsticks to complete the Asian illusion. In truth, Quartez had been born in south Florida. But again: appearances. Spider moved away from the stairs and found an empty space near the back. As he sat down to wait out her conversation with the K-Corp suits, he noticed that Satoshi was laying on the table before the men. She was nude, but she had rolls of sushi and slices of vegetables covering her nipples, stomach, and pubic area. Spider shook his head. Sushi in the raw wasn't his cup of tea. He waited patiently until Quartez had finished with the suits and turned to walk away.

Quartez

When she did, he whistled loudly as she made her way to the stairs, catching the attention of the suits at the table. Quartez narrowed her eyes at him as she crossed the room and joined him at his table. "What the hell are you thinking?" she hissed at him. "Don't blow this deal for me. You know how the Kobiyashi reps feel about you."

"You wanted to see me?" Spider asked, ignoring her question. Then he smiled. "And fuck Kobiyashi. You can quote me on that, by the way."

Quartez shook her head and grunted at him. "Why do I put up with you, you lowly little sewer rat?" she muttered in Mandarin, knowing that Spider could understand her perfectly.

"Because I bring in the dough," Spider replied in Russian. "And you know it," he finished in English.

"You've got a call from upstairs."

"We are upstairs. *You* are upstairs."

"Not me. *Her.*" Quartez stared hard at him. "She wants to talk to you. Looks like you've got another one."

Spider shook his head. "That's it? I thought you had some work for me."

"This is work, and you know it. Whether or not you get paid is up to her." Quartez stood up and glared at him. "Now get back to your little rat hole," she said in Spanish. Her glare became a smile and she switched back to English. "And if I were you, I'd get rid of that suit. You smell like a fucking garbage dump." She giggled that high, annoying giggle to herself, then turned and walked away from him, disappearing down the stairs.

Spider had a moment where he wanted to regale her K-Corp boys with tales of the old Quartez. The days when her name had been Diana and she had been a nobody whore on Desperation Avenue, long before the Cat O' Nine Club had fallen into her possession by less than legal means. But he held it in check. His alliance with Quartez was always uneasy, and it always would be, but it was necessary. He needed a place to operate, and Quartez needed the extra cash. Her twenty percent cut was better than nothing.

Spider left the table behind, smiling to himself as the K-Corp boys quieted down when he walked past them, and took the stairs to the second floor. Upon seeing Bridgit behind the bar, he was tempted to skip the God conversation and have another drink instead. He could listen to her talk about nothing all night, as long as she did it in that voice of hers. But business, good or bad, had to come first. And Quartez, as much as he disliked her, was right. He had to get out of this fucking suit.

He crossed the second floor, passing a cigar bar with a perfect view of the stage. The scent of Cubans caught his nose, and he was tempted once more. He had a stash in the Hive, and if he really felt like it, he could grab one and come back here. He moved on. There was a steel door set into the wall about thirty feet from the cigar bar. Spider stopped when he reached this door, and his right hand moved to a small keypad set into the wall just beside the door. Spider punched a complicated sequence of numbers into the machine and the door popped open with barely a sound. Spider went through and eased the door shut behind him.

Now he was standing outside on a catwalk several feet above an alley that ran behind the club. Below, he could see a few of the girls standing outside, and he could smell their Russian cigarettes. The club's backlights illuminated most of the alley, and he could see a body several feet from the club's back entrance. Another wannabe rapist. Every few weeks, there was some new asshole who tried to pull something on the girls while they stood outside and smoked and tried to relax for a few minutes. He wished the girls would let one of these guys live. How else was everybody supposed to find out that the girls all carried pulse-pistols when they stood outside? Quartez had made it a requirement for employment after too many of her girls had been raped, and a few killed, while smoking in this alley.

Spider gave a short whistle, and one of the girls looked up. He saw that it was Vinyssa, and he gave her a smile. Then he pointed to the body. "What happened, Vin? Another punk try to get handsy with you?"

Vinyssa shook her blond head and said, "Nah, it was Dauphine. She was out here like an hour ago and the guy came out of nowhere. Two in the chest and one in the head."

Spider shook his head. "Has anybody called Finnegan?"

"Not that I know of."

"Well, get in there and call him up. Get that body out of here before Quartez comes out and sees it. You know what she'll do to you, Vin. And to Dauphine. And you too, Renada." Spider pointed to the girl standing next to Vinyssa, a raven-haired beauty in her own right. "Make the call."

Vinyssa saluted him, and Spider caught another whiff of her Russian cigarette. Definitely off-brand, and probably not even real. "Yes sir, Commandant," Vinyssa said.

Spider walked across the catwalk to the next building, where a door identical to the one he had passed through inside the club waited for him. He punched a different combination of numbers into an identical keypad and waited while the door hissed open. Immediately, his ears were assaulted with loud drum-and-bass music that pounded inside his head like sledgehammers. Spider grimaced and shut the door behind him, then shouted, "Turn that shit off, Severen!"

The music's volume immediately lowered, but it did not terminate. The Hive was dark, and Spider knew what had been going on while he had been gone. Instead of mentioning it, he simply walked down the spiral staircase in front of him to the first floor and sat down on a ratty sofa. "Now," he began, "I said turn the music off, Severen."

The music ceased.

"Thank you," Spider said. Before he could continue, a female voice called from the darkness: "What is that smell? Is that you, boss?"

"Yes, I fell in some garbage when these Triad punks tried to rob me and yes, I know the suit is probably ruined and yes, it was an Idio Nagata original. Now can we move on?"

Banks of fluorescent lights began to click on around him. Spider knew the state in which he would find his team.

Severen stood behind his computer terminal, holding a large Nerf IG9000 in both hands, his luminescent tattoos shining beneath his white T-shirt. Behind him stood Thrash, who wore a pair of black and green goggles on her head. They accentuated her slicked-back black dreadlocks and the earrings she wore, made from broken microprocessors. She held an identical Nerf cannon in her hands. Behind her were banks of servers and routers and a host of other equipment that Spider secretly had no idea about. His job was to run the team.

"Sorry, boss," Thrash blurted. "We got bored while you were gone. No work, you know?"

Thrash and Severen

"Maybe we have some now. Whoever gets a line with God the quickest gets to go into the club for half an hour. Loser goes for dinner. Who wants it?"

The two techs dropped their Nerf weapons to the ground and scrambled to their identical terminals. Thrash brought up a file and moused through several lines until she clicked on one. As "Holiday in Cambodia" began to stream through speakers built into the ceiling, Spider smiled on the couch. Thrash at least knew how to kiss his ass while he waited. The tech monkeys busied themselves with trying to find God at this time of night. Spider waited patiently for exactly three and a half minutes before Severen shouted, "Got her!"

"Fuck you," Thrash said, pushing herself away from her terminal. "I was almost there."

"Almost doesn't cut it," Severen teased. "Now go get me some dumplings." He grinned. "And noodles."

As Thrash stood up, Spider snapped his fingers at her. "Sit your ass down, Thrash. Nobody goes anywhere until this is done."

"But I'm hungry," Severen complained.

"Wait. Is she talking?"

Severen turned back to his screen and punched several keys. He waited a few seconds, then got a response. "She's up. You're disturbing her tea, apparently."

"I don't give a shit."

"You want me to tell her that?"

"No. Tell her I need a face to face. Now."

"On it." Severen typed several lines of text, then waited. He got an immediate reply. "She's ready when you are, boss."

Spider pointed to a large screen hanging over the server banks. "Bring her up on the big guy."

Severen typed another few lines, then waited.

Spider turned his attention to the screen. He didn't enjoy this kind of work, but he figured it was the price he had to pay for doing business with her once in a while. God worked in mysterious ways, but it didn't always mean he liked it. Helping refugees was never in the cards for him, but somehow, he had fallen into it. There was little to no money in it, but sometimes, it was good to give his people the practice. And if he didn't feel like it, he could always pass it down the line. Maybe CoreData would take it. That guy was always hard up for cash. Not surprising when you had an affinity for hookers. Or maybe the Ice

Lady. She didn't mind working for little to no money, and she was just as good by herself as his team was together.

There was a flicker on the screen, and then he was on a video conference with God.

She wore a red silk kimono with green dragons and other designs that were not readily identifiable. The kimono matched her bright red hair and accented her pale skin. Her green eyes seemed to bore through Spider the way they always did. As usual, the camera was pointed at a bare white wall, giving no clue to her location. "What do you want, Spider?" Her voice echoed through the Hive. "Why couldn't we do this over IRC?"

"Because I want to know why you're giving me another one only three days after the last one. Don't you have other people that handle this shit for you? Considering that I don't get paid, and neither does my team, I'm not so sure—"

God interrupted him. "I had this set up with someone else. But he's dead now. Someone got to him. I had to reroute this one as quick as I could, and you were the only one that I knew I could … trust with this." She seemed to have trouble with that word *trust*. "Satisfied?"

"Who was the contact?"

"I guess it doesn't matter now, since he's dead. Victor Trace."

Spider knew the name. Everyone in his business did. Trace was a master forger, one of the best in the business. He could do almost anything: passports, visas, new IDs. Spider had no idea he was part of the network.

"Jesus. What happened?"

"Details are still sketchy, even for me. My informant hasn't called back yet."

Spider ran a hand through his hair and looked down. "I don't know, God—"

The redhead grunted in frustration. "You know I hate that name—"

"I don't like using your name on here. The same way you're not using my name, either."

"Then call me Cyber. You know that."

"Whatever you say, God." Her arrogance astounded him sometimes, and he always let her know it in subtle ways. "Now tell me about this refugee."

"She's not a refugee. Same deal as last time. She's about five minutes outside the Red right now. She's riding in a JR Cab, serial number 434RJF. She'll be there in half an hour if the traffic holds."

"I thought we were disturbing your tea."

The redhead smiled. "You are. I multitask, you know." She winked at him. "Because I'm smart."

Smart was an understatement, and Spider knew it just as much as she did. God, or Cyber, or the Internet Angel, or the Keyboard Queen, or The Cyber Princess, or whatever you wanted to call her, was a legend. If the rumors were true, she was only thirty-one years old, but had an IQ over 200. She was responsible for hacking the FBI database and erasing her own file. Ditto the NSA. And she was behind some of the greatest hacks in history: the FAA Shutdown in 2018, the NORAD Hack of 2021, and many others that were almost too good to be true. If Spider didn't know her personally, he wouldn't believe any of it. But based on what he knew, he figured at least half of it was on the level, maybe more. Her name was Elizabeth Wilder, and she was the world's most famous, and most reviled, super-hacker.

"So tell me what you know," Spider said.

"Not much. She'll be wearing an old Thundercats T-shirt. That's your signal. She's got blond hair and a tattoo on her forearm of a rose wrapped in a chain. She told me her name was Jennifer, but it isn't."

"What is it?"

"If she feels like telling you, Spider, she will. Otherwise, let it go. I ran facial-recognition on her from our conversation. She is who she says she is, okay? Even if she doesn't want me or you to know her name. Just get her to the Surgeon and bring her back. Two hours, max. You'll get paid this time—"

"Is that a promise?"

"It's a commitment. Understand? Now, two things. One, do not fuck with this girl, Spider. If you do, I will find out about it and I will castrate you—"

"Yeah, yeah, I get it. No funny business."

"Second, do not lose the implant this time, got it? I want it. For the collection."

"You're sick, you know that?"

"Do as you're told, and you'll see some green this time. I have to go. My tea is getting cold. Remember what I said. Call me when she gets there. I want to make sure she's okay." The screen turned to static for a moment before it went blank. Thrash typed in a command and the screen shut itself off.

Spider crossed his arms as he turned away from the blank screen and faced his team. "Get Takashi in here, pronto," he said. "I want him running security during the meeting. Tell him to bring that custom pulse-pistol of his." Severen went to work immediately, tapping keys at his terminal. Spider turned to Thrash. "Pull up the coordinates on that cab. Track it and let me know the second it arrives outside. If it deviates, call me. If it stops anywhere but here, call me." He turned away from his team and headed for the stairs. "I'll be in the club."

"Got a date, boss?" Thrash teased.

"Something like that," Spider muttered as he began to ascend the stairs. He swung the heavy door open and stepped out into the night.

4

TWENTY MINUTES LATER, Spider was zipping up his pants and kissing Bridgit on the cheek. The bathroom stall was cramped and rather dirty, but neither party seemed to mind. Bridgit smoothed down her black cocktail dress and smiled at him. "Better than last time," she muttered, brushing his cheek with her lips. "You stuck the dismount perfectly."

Spider grinned at her through his endorphin high and said, "We should try it in a proper bed next time. These stalls are cramping my style."

"You didn't show it much," Bridgit teased.

Before Spider could reply, his smartphone rang inside his jacket pocket. He lifted the jacket from a hook on the back of the stall door and dug into the pocket. "Yeah?" he answered, knowing without hearing a word what the call was for.

"She's here," Thrash responded. "She's … it looks like she's smoking a cigarette under the canopy outside. Just standing in the rain."

Spider nodded. "Apprehensive. They all are. Give her a few minutes. If she doesn't come in, send one of the girls out to bring her up. You know where I'll be."

"In your lair, like usual," said Thrash, and disconnected the call.

Spider slipped his jacket back on, catching a whiff of the garbage smell once more, then buttoned the front and swung the stall door open. He turned back to Bridgit and smiled at her. "You were amazing."

"So were you."

They shared a brief kiss, followed by Bridgit adjusting her strapless bra beneath her dress. Then both left the stall and headed for the door. A man in a black suit with pale skin stood at the sink, washing his hands. Spider gave the man a wink as he escorted Bridgit out the door and back into the club.

They had ducked into a bathroom only a few feet from the bar. Spider saw Marisol behind the cedar, mixing drinks. Then Bridgit slipped into a hidden opening in the bar, and suddenly she was on the other side. She ran one hand over Spider's left arm and said, "Find me later, okay?"

Spider nodded, and touched her cheek with his hand. Then he turned and disappeared into the smoky air of the club, passing a large Chinese man in a gray suit and a white man wearing sunglasses. He weaved through the crowd of people gathered at the edge overlooking the stage. His eye caught a glimpse of Dauphine on the stage, dressed in her Red Riding Hood outfit. She danced away from Leonetta, who was dressed as a sexy Big Bad Wolf. The two woman intertwined briefly and shared a short kiss, then they broke apart and danced to opposite ends of the stage. Spider turned away as the crowd hooted and hollered and begged for more. Dauphine knew how to lay it on thick.

He found his usual table across the club. He had chosen it mainly for the view it offered of the stairs and the rest of the club. There were no doors on this side, no way for anyone to sneak in behind him and get the drop on him. In his line of work, that was always a concern. Spider sat down in his usual chair and before he could even wave his hand in the air, Marisol was there, holding the bottle of Chivas and a glass that he had been about to request. Marisol set the glass down and filled it from the bottle, then set the open bottle next to the glass. Spider gave her a pat on the ass and sent her on her way.

His eyes found the stage once more. Dauphine was giving herself to the Big Bad Wolf, letting the Wolf take her in every possible way. Spider smirked and thought, *that's no way to get to Grandmother's house.* He sipped his Chivas and let his eyes roam the club.

Down below, he could see several tables filled with steampunks, admiring each other's glittering clockwork and copper-plated hearts. To the left of the 'punks were a group of tech monkeys, hogging the club's free WiFi for their own uses. Each one was glued to a tablet or laptop, the glow from the screen casting eerie shadows on their faces. Spider thought, not for the first time, about what a melting pot the Red had become in the last few years. The District itself was not much older than that, in fact, but since its inception, it had become a boomtown on its own, if you knew where to look. Barely anything in the Red was legal in the outside world, but here, where cops feared to tread, nothing was outside the realm of possibility. Black-market EBMs, illegal body-mods, guns, drugs, grey-market software (and hardware), hot cars, hot music players … the list went on and on. Here, everything and everyone had a price. Nothing was taboo.

Spider's eyes flicked over to the stairwell, as they usually did, but he found nothing. As he was reaching for his smartphone to call Thrash, the device began to ring and vibrate inside his jacket pocket. He knew what the call was for, but he answered it anyway. "She inside?"

"Yep," answered Severen. "She's talking to Quartez right now. Should be heading your way in thirty seconds."

"Where's Takashi?"

"On the way up. He just got here not even a minute ago."

"Got it," Spider said, and hung up the phone. He slid one hand beneath the table and felt along the bottom for the pulse-pistol. It was still there, just as it had always been. The feel of it against his palm was comforting. If something went bad, he needed a way out, and this was it. One shot from the pulse-pistol would blow a hole the size of a fist in someone's chest. He slid the weapon out of its holster and inspected it, chambering a round. Then he slid the gun back into its hidden holster and took another sip of Chivas.

His eyes flicked towards the stairs, where an unremarkable Japanese man, dressed in a black pinstripe suit with expensive shoes, was cresting the top step. The man's eyes darted around the club, instantly taking in everything around him. When his eyes alighted on Spider, he made no indication of recognition with his eyes or body. Instead, he simply crossed the club and took a seat in front of Spider.

Spider signaled Marisol for two more glasses, which were delivered almost instantly. Marisol disappeared behind the bar when the job was done, as if she had never been there in the first place. Spider poured a glass of Chivas for the Japanese man and slid it across the table to him. "Thanks for coming in on such short notice," he said.

"No problem," said the Japanese man, after taking a sip from his glass. "I was in the neighborhood already."

"Medicine man again?"

The Japanese man nodded, and took another sip of Chivas. "Grandmother insists on it." He took a sniff of the air. "Is that you?"

"Yeah, it's me. Met some garbage on the way here earlier. They ruined my suit."

Takashi took a sip of his drink, but remained silent.

Spider sipped his own glass of liquor, then said, "I've got a refugee coming in right now. Usual gig, but this time we get paid. So says God."

The Japanese man nodded, but said nothing. After a moment, he sipped his drink.

Spider continued. "Surgeon and back again. Think you can handle it?"

"You don't pay me to watch cartoons."

"That I don't. Shouldn't be more than two hours."

The Japanese man nodded again. Spider refilled his own glass and held the bottle up to the Japanese man, who waved it away. "Something wrong, Takashi?"

Takashi shook his head. "Just thinking."

Spider set the bottle down nearby. "You know what happens when you think, right?"

Takashi nodded solemnly and stood up, buttoning his suit jacket. "Time to work, boss. We're on the clock."

Takashi and "Jennifer"

Spider looked past him and saw a blond girl who looked barely old enough to drink alcohol at a Blue District bar as she topped the stairs. In the club's meager light, Spider could make out the Thundercats T-shirt she wore, Lion-O with his sword raised and ready to do battle with Mum-Ra. The tattoo that God had mentioned stood out in the club's half-light; a rose wrapped in chains on her forearm. Her hair was pulled back in a loose ponytail and she wore an expression of mild terror on her face. Spider wondered if she had ever been in a club like this before, or if the terror on her face was simply a reflection of her current situation. Spider had heard all the stories, knew all the angles and all the responses, but every time he met one, he was floored. Most of them had been through something that he himself could never fathom. He wasn't sure if he believed it entirely, but he knew that something was happening to these people, and it terrified them.

Takashi took his customary place behind Spider's right shoulder, hands clasped in front of him but ready for action at the slightest provocation. Takashi, like Spider, had learned that just because God vetted somebody didn't necessarily mean they were who they said they were. Even God could be fooled once in a while, and had. It was better to be prepared than caught off-guard.

The blond made her way slowly through the VIP area towards Spider, her eyes darting back and forth. Spider had seen this type of hyper-vigilance before, mostly in veterans. But it was present in nearly every human being who had suffered severe trauma. It was one more thing that helped establish the girl's bonafides. It was something that was not easy to fake. The girl walked cautiously towards him, her hands clutching each other hard enough to break skin. By the time she made it to the table, Spider could see the stress-lines on her face and the bags beneath her eyes. What was odd to him, what made him stop and think, was that the girl was beautiful, despite those things. She had flowing blond hair that was cut just above her shoulders, and her eyes seemed to have a sparkle contained within, dimmed only slightly by what she had been through.

Spider put on his softest face and focused his eyes on the girl. "Jennifer?"

The blond nodded, then cast her eyes to the floor for a moment. When she raised them once more, there was a hardness there that Spider had missed upon first glance. But then again, considering what the girl had been through, she'd have to be tough to still be alive. He had read countless stories and heard even more from God and a few other people about the suicide rate among people with this girl's … affliction. And the hoops she'd had to jump through to get where she was right now … it was a lot to take in, but Spider knew more than most about it, and he knew what to say and how to say it.

"It's okay. You're safe here." He indicated the seat that Takashi had only recently vacated. "Please sit down."

Jennifer sat down in the offered chair, clasping her hands primly in front of her. She would meet his gaze for only a second or two before she would turn away. Spider poured a generous amount of Chivas into the third glass and slid it across the table to her. "Drink it. It'll help. Trust me."

Jennifer didn't speak. She simply nodded and accepted the offered glass. The contents disappeared down her throat in one swallow, and she set the empty glass on the table. Spider refilled it and capped the bottle. "Feel better?"

Jennifer did not answer immediately. Instead, her eyes roamed the club while she sipped her second glass. Then she looked at him and asked, "How do you do this?"

"Do what?"

"Live with this. I saw someone get shot in the face on the way here. On the street. Like it was nothing. How do you live with that every day?"

Spider glanced up at Takashi for a moment. The Japanese man would not return his gaze. He didn't have to. His silence was all the permission Spider needed. He reached forward and took Jennifer's hands in his. "You wanna know the truth?"

Jennifer nodded.

"We don't. We all die a little bit every day when we see something like that. All of us. Everybody that lives here, everybody that works here, everybody who has ever tried to build a life here and failed. It's the price we pay. We're all hard." He hooked a thumb at Takashi. "See this guy here? He's seen more shit than I ever will. And it's made him tough. Impenetrable. But he's in there still. Just buried deep down inside." He met Jennifer's eyes for a moment. "Just like I am. And just like you are, Jennifer."

The girl held his gaze for another second, then looked away, her eyes roaming over the club's patrons. "Kimber," she muttered, so low that Spider almost missed it with the club's noise surrounding him. "My name is Kimber. I just … I didn't know how dangerous this would be, so I lied about my name."

Spider shook his head. "You don't have to tell me anything you don't want to, okay?" Then he smiled. "Kimber, huh? Like the Hologram?"

The girl eyed him and asked, "Who?"

Spider waved his hand. "Never mind. Not important." Then he downed his glass. "Now, on to business. We have certain protocols that we have to follow." He stood up and held out his hand to her. "Are you ready to meet God?"

Kimber took the offered hand and stood up. "I think so." Spider smiled at her, doing his best to soothe her. She had already been through something that Spider could never comprehend on an emotional level. He had read enough on the subject to understand it academically, but that was it. He had no way of knowing what the girl's current emotional state was, other than her outward appearance, which wasn't good. Takashi followed close behind as Spider led her through the VIP area to the door, his door. Takashi kept an eye out while Spider punched in his code and swung the door open.

Red District air whooshed through the opening, filling Spider's nose with the scents of his city: cigarette smoke, car exhaust, fried meats, fresh vegetables, and just a hint of marijuana. He breathed it in deeply. He loved it. He hated the way the Red was, but he loved the way it smelled. Such were the complexities of his character.

Spider led Kimber through the door, then closed it once Takashi joined them. The three crossed the catwalk, their steps echoing through the alley. Spider looked down and saw Finnegan, bigger than hell, lifting that body from the ground and throwing it over his shoulder. He glanced up at the sound of footsteps, then relaxed slightly when he saw Spider.

"You got this, Finnegan?" Spider asked the large man.

A nod, then the big man answered with, "No sweat, Spider. You're looking slick tonight. Nice suit."

Spider chuckled and shook his head. "Don't mention the suit. Long story, Finn. Go up to the VIP area and have a drink when you're finished. Tell Marisol I said so."

Finnegan gave Spider a salute. "Thanks, Spider. Take it easy."

"Yeah, have a good one, Finnegan."

They had reached the door now, and Spider punched in his code. Takashi brought up the rear as the three entered the building. Spider closed the door behind them and made sure the lock engaged, then he turned to Kimber and smiled. "Welcome to the Hive," he said, and spread his arms. "This is where we do business. Last stop before we get that thing out of you, okay?"

Kimber nodded, but said nothing.

Spider led the way down the spiral staircase to the bottom floor. He introduced Thrash and Severen, then instructed his tech monkeys to get in touch with God and bring her up on the big screen. He made sure to use certain key words in his commands that told Thrash he wanted facial-recognition run on the new arrival as soon as a camera could be rotated in place to snap a picture. Thrash complied, while Severen busied himself with contacting God over IRC.

"She's ready, boss," Severen said after a few moments. "Say the word."

He looked to Thrash, giving her a few seconds before he asked, "Got it?"

Thrash nodded and turned away from her screen to face him. "She's good, just like God said. Everything's in order. All yours, boss."

Spider took his place before the large screen, keeping Kimber on his left. The screen switched on, and there was the customary burst of high-energy static, then the screen flickered. After a few seconds, it stabilized and God was smiling down at him.

"Jennifer," God began, "are you okay? Did you have any problems?"

The girl shook her head. "No. I'm fine."

"And how are you being treated? Nobody's tried to pull anything, right?" God turned her eyes to Spider and glared at him. "I mean him, specifically."

"No. He's been very nice."

"Good." God cleared her throat, then continued. "I've already contacted your Surgeon, Jennifer. He's only a few blocks away from you, and he's waiting. Are you ready?"

The girl nodded.

"Then let's get that out of you." She turned her gaze to Spider. "You know what to do?"

"Aye-aye, God."

"Don't call me that. Get her there and get her back, understand? No fuck-ups this time."

"I've got my best guy here."

"Good. Take care of this, Spider. I mean it." Then her face softened and she turned her gaze back to the girl. "Jennifer, you take care of yourself. I'll speak with you again when this is all over, okay?"

"Okay."

"Call me when it's done," God said, addressing this to Spider.

"Yes, mother," Spider said, then glanced at Severen. "Cut her."

"Hey!" God shouted, but the transmission cut off and the screen went dark.

Spider chuckled softly to himself. That ought to burn her little pale redheaded ass. Sometimes she needed a good reminder that he was doing her a favor, one for which he expected to be paid. He turned to Takashi, who was standing a few feet behind him. "You pack your jazz?"

Takashi nodded.

"Good. You know what to do if something happens. Get her there as fast as you can."

Another nod.

Spider switched his gaze to Kimber, who was trying to hide her fear beneath a mask of resolve. "Kimber? It's okay. This is Takashi." He indicated the Japanese man. "He's going to take you down the street exactly eight blocks to the Surgeon. You'll be there for two hours, at the absolute max. Then it's over, okay?"

"Just get it out of me," Kimber said, trying to keep the pleading out of her voice.

"Don't worry." He turned back to Takashi. "God's watching."

"She always is."

Spider led them up the stairs to the door. Takashi would take her through the club and out the front door. If he was lucky, he could find a cab. If not, he'd have to walk her the eight blocks. Either way, it wouldn't be easy. Spider silently wished them both good luck, then punched in his code and opened the door.

"We'll be watching you both, okay? Takashi has a transmitter in his jacket that'll let us know if you go off-course. Stay with him and he'll get you there."

Kimber nodded.

"Off you go." He closed the door behind them, then took the staircase back to the first floor. He leaned over Thrash's terminal, only inches away from her. "You got them?"

"I got 'em. Heading through the club to the front door."

"Good. Tak will switch the GPS on when he hits the street. When they get there, hand them over to Severen, then take five and grab us some dinner." He turned away and shook his head. "I'm gonna change out of this ruined piece of shit and take a shower. Come get me if there's a problem."

"Will do, boss."

As Spider turned away from his team, he could hear Severen cranking up the dance music once more. He wondered if it wasn't a direct feed from the club. Then he disappeared into the back of the Hive, where the living quarters were, thinking about which suit he wanted to put on after his shower.

5

TAKASHI CAUGHT A whiff of cigarette smoke as he escorted Kimber out the front door and switched on the tiny GPS locator hidden in his pants pocket. Two hookers were hanging around the club's entrance, smoking Chinese cigarettes while they attempted to dissuade potential customers from the club by offering the real thing. Takashi pushed his way past them, nearly shoving Kimber in front of him. "What—" she began, but Takashi cut her off. "Keep moving," he said.

They walked down Desperation Avenue toward the next intersection. Valencia Drive loomed ahead of them and flashing neon told them to stop and wait. Takashi kept Kimber close to him and slightly behind as they approached, his other hand inside his jacket on the grip of his pulse-pistol. He didn't expect any trouble, but that didn't mean there would be none.

The light changed and suddenly the crowd surged forward, all jockeying to get across the street in the twenty seconds that the sign allowed. Takashi felt a cyberpunk brush against his shoulder, then the 'punk was gone. Ahead, he could see people lining up outside a club called Eye Candy while a doorman, bigger than Finnegan, kept them all in check. Takashi maneuvered the girl past the line and kept moving.

Seven blocks now. Takashi kept hold of Kimber, making sure she didn't get separated from him in the surging crowds. At this time of night, they were lucky to be on the sidewalk. Takashi could see pedestrians walking in the street gutters, ignoring the waste and rainwater that swept towards overflowing storm drains. A cab's horn honked to his right, followed by the angry snarl of a driver as he shook his fist at the cab in front of him. He heard a ruckus across Desperation Avenue, and turned his head slightly to see two Japanese men in the middle of a street brawl with what looked like two Hispanics. Takashi turned away and kept his focus.

The next intersection was less crowded. J-Pop princesses and Tokyo fashion hounds stood, waiting for the light to change. Takashi picked out a few hookers in the small crowd, along with two pick-pockets who were silently robbing an oblivious blond woman. An info-junkie leaned against the street post, his head only a few inches below the flashing sign. When it changed, Takashi followed the crowd across the street.

Six blocks.

Takashi swept his eyes left to right, staying vigilant. Every person he saw was a potential threat, whether to him or the girl. Everybody wanted something here, and few had any qualms about stealing or killing to get it. He chanced a quick look to his left, eyeing the girl. For her part, she seemed to be taking it all in stride. Nothing about her expression betrayed any emotion. She was a blank slate as they moved through the Red to the Surgeon.

Takashi, like Spider, spent an inordinate amount of time dismissing the truth behind the … refugees' stories. He used euphemisms and words like "refugee" to describe the people that he came into contact with in this aspect of his job. He had long ago tossed out any belief he may have attached to their accounts. That was science fiction, plain and simple. Takashi was in the business of making money, and he had a very specific skill set which aided him in that pursuit. He had used those skills to make money as a bodyguard for many years now, and not always in the employ of Spider. The Red had a need for people like him.

He pushed past these thoughts and focused on the job. To the Surgeon and back. Two hours max.

Movement on his right caught his eye. His grip tightened on the pulse-pistol, but soon relaxed as he saw it was nothing more than a hooker using a cigarette lighter shaped like an old handgun. The hooker flashed him a trademark smile as he moved past her. A door opened on his left, and a group of tattooed Orange District Power Authority workers, drunk beyond words, stumbled out of Lenny's Brew House and into the street, all smiles and laughter. The bar's doorman kept a watchful eye on the group as they crossed the street into traffic. There was a squeal of brakes, followed by several car horns and one screaming cabby.

Takashi kept his eyes on the sidewalk ahead of him.

Another intersection was approaching: Yevgeny Street. The light was currently green, so he hustled the refugee along ahead of him. They melted into a crowd of motorheads as they began to cross the street, and Takashi could smell motor oil and burnt rubber emanating from each one. He closed off his nose to the smells.

Five blocks.

Takashi led the girl around a couple of needle-junkies shooting up against the outside wall of a Japanese tea house. One of the junkies looked up at him as he passed, and Takashi saw the familiar vacant-eyed expression on the man's face that he had seen countless times before. The Red was rife with drug abuse. Los Pistoleros, the city's Hispanic gang, controlled nearly ninety percent of the drug trade, and much of that flowed through the Red District on its way to the city.

Up the block, he could see what looked like a car accident. There was a body lying on the sidewalk in a pool of blood. The pedestrian traffic simply wove its way around the scene, most of the people not even giving it a second look or thought. A Mil City Cab had struck a pedestrian trying to cross in traffic, it looked like. Takashi kept a tight grip on Kimber's arm as they made their way past the scene.

He stopped underneath a street post, staring at the flashing crosswalk sign above his head. He waited for as long as he could, thirty seconds, then he wrapped one hand around Kimber's forearm and said, "Come on." He stepped out into traffic, ignoring the horn blasts and middle fingers he received.

Across the street, he loosened his grip on Kimber. "What's wrong?" she asked him.

"I have a bad feeling. Keep moving." He sped up. Only four blocks now.

Takashi could gradually feel a bass beat in the soles of his feet as they moved up the street. He found the source when he and the girl passed in front of one the Red District's most outrageous dance clubs, The Jade Serpent. There was the usual absurd line to get in on his left. He kept Kimber on his right and shouldered other pedestrians out of his way. The beat he could feel in his feet was a J-Pop song that he vaguely recognized, but he couldn't place it. The doorman outside gave Takashi a nod of recognition which he did not return, then opened the door to let in more of the Red District's finest citizens.

The J-Pop song and its beat began to fade as he moved on, keeping one hand on Kimber's arm.

As they approached an alley so small it didn't have a name, Takashi's hair stood up and he felt a prickling sensation along his spine. He was turning to warn Kimber of an impending attack when he felt the weighted sap hit the back of his head. He stumbled and went down to his knees, losing his grip on Kimber. She screamed, but it was short-lived. Takashi could hear at least two more attackers take hold of her and cover her mouth. He felt himself being dragged into the alley by his feet, and he could feel the grease and grime of the Red District as it rubbed itself into his suit.

His feet were dropped to the asphalt, then he was rolled over onto his side. Still in a daze from the sap, he could feel someone begin to dig through his pockets. This snapped him out of his stupor, but he kept still.

Kimber mumbled something, then Takashi heard a low, maniacal laugh. "Looks like we got us a piece of fresh meat tonight, boys." The Japanese man turned his head to the left ever so slightly and caught sight of a thin white man with a shaved head and a Swastika tattooed on his chest. He wore no shirt. Instead, the garment was tucked into the back pocket of his dirty jeans. Black combat boots with steel toes completed the outfit, and Takashi knew immediately who he was dealing with. The Snowmen. They were the only white-power gang in the city. They controlled the illegal body-mod trade and a sliver of the drug trade, mostly crystal and K.

Takashi heard a second voice, this one higher in pitch, answer: "I love fresh meat. And she's so pretty." He could hear Kimber's struggles, could hear her fighting to keep away from them. He remained still.

"Shouldn't wander around here with some chink businessman for an escort, little girl," said the first voice.

Now that the voice had spoken again, Takashi was able to confirm in his head that it was Ephram Hallker, a local lieutenant in the Snowmen. Takashi smiled. He was a guy who should know better than to yank tourists off Desperation Avenue during peak business hours. Dead tourists didn't spend money. Live tourists came back again, usually the next night. Takashi dismissed the racial slur out of hand. Hallker was an idiot, and he couldn't help it. Not that it mattered.

Finally, the third voice that Takashi knew was there spoke up. It was a woman. "When you two are finished with her, I'd like a turn, too."

"Well hell, why didn't you say so?" said the second voice. It was filled with excitement now. "I wouldn't mind seeing that. Here, I'll get her legs."

And Kimber began to scream once more.

Takashi waited a few seconds, using the time to judge distances and angles. He didn't want there to be any mistakes.

The second voice was the closest to him at the moment. He could see a pair of black Wez Crater combat-style boots with a greasy sock above each one. The legs attached to the boots did not look large, and the body did not either. Kimber's shaking form could be seen just in front of these legs, her lower back against the asphalt.

The first voice, he could see, was seven feet away from the second voice on the right, and preparing to drop those dirty jeans to the ground. Takashi wasn't worried about Ephram Hallker. The third voice, the woman, was wearing the same boots as Hallker, and she was standing about four feet away on the left. She might be a problem. Takashi could see strong legs and a well-built upper body. If his plan worked, it wouldn't matter.

Before he could act, there was a shout from the second voice, and Takashi saw Kimber's head withdraw from the man's crotch. As he began to crumble, Takashi stood up and wrapped one arm around the man's throat, yanking the custom pulse-pistol from beneath his jacket. Kimber rolled away and ducked behind a stack of broken pallets. Takashi immediately fired at the woman, hitting her twice in the chest and blowing her wide open.

She dropped to the ground as Hallker began to draw his own weapon.

Takashi fired again, twice. The blasts took Hallker's head off, splattering it against the grimy brick wall behind the now-headless body. The corpse twitched once then toppled to the ground, spilling blood in a growing pool.

Now Takashi spun the man in his grip around, then kicked him into the wall where his boss's brains were now cooling. The man tried to duck away, but the pulse-pistol rounds caught him in the ribs, blowing his side open. He collapsed, still clutching his side, and bled out in seconds.

Takashi holstered the pulse-pistol and began to search for Kimber.

She had hidden herself between the stack of pallets and the brick wall they leaned against. It took him several seconds to locate her because she made no sound. He couldn't even detect her breathing. When he coaxed her out, she expelled air in a whooshing breath, and he realized she had been holding it in the entire time.

"Are you hurt?" he asked.

Kimber shook her head. "No. I'm fine."

"Good." Takashi turned away from her and began to search the bodies. He found his wallet as well as several hundred dollars in cash, which he pocketed. When he rejoined Kimber, who waited for him near the mouth of the alley, she asked, "Did you just rob them?"

"That one—" Takashi pointed. "—stole my wallet. Now I have it back. Are you ready?"

She nodded.

"Let's go." He tapped the device in his ear. "Anybody copy?"

"I got you, Tak." It was Thrash. "Closed channel too, lover. What's up?"

"I'm working, Thrash. Just went off-course for a few minutes. Did you notice?"

"I did. Figured you went off to cheat on me with that lovely little abductee."

"Not on your life. Just had a run-in with Ephram Hallker and the Snowmen. Hallker's down and so are his minions."

"You okay, baby?"

"I'm fine. So is the girl. Take me off the closed channel, Thrash. We'll talk when I get back."

"Whatever you say, lover." There was a hiss of static, then Thrash said. "You're back on the main channel, Tak."

"Good. I'm moving on now."

Back on the street, Takashi joined a group of circuiters, their bodies covered in bits of wiring and fiber-optic lights and plastic tubes. They were heading, he knew, for a place called The Wire Jockey up the block. The bar catered to their specific fetish more than any other place in the Red. Takashi found these thoughts drifting through his mind as he kept one eye on Kimber and the other on the group ahead of him.

They crossed the street, along with the circuiters and a motley collection of the Red's inhabitants, including a priest, and Takashi told himself that he only had three blocks now.

He stayed behind the circuiters until the group reached The Wire Jockey, almost at the next intersection. The blocks were getting longer now as they moved farther into the Red. He led Kimber around the rowdy group as they laughed and filed into the bar one by one. Moving on, Takashi dodged around couples who waited outside an adult movie theater. He moved Kimber down the street towards the next intersection.

Takashi waited for the light this time, but only because it took no longer than fifteen seconds. He knew he would be dodging the Bazaar next.

He crossed the street with Kimber at his side. He held her arm now only to keep her close. He knew she wouldn't stray after what had just happened. He wasn't worried about that now. He had other concerns.

The Chadworth-Inkwell Bazaar was called simply the Bazaar by those who lived here. It was named this because it extended down Desperation Avenue from the intersection of Chadworth to the next intersection of Inkwell. Roof-top farmers selling their organic wares to the public, jewelry makers with their creations laid out before them, butchers selling cuts of various legal and illegal meats, grey-market dealers hawking whatever software or hardware they could scrounge up to make a few dollars.

Takashi hustled Kimber past all of this, and past a gun dealer situated behind a booth filled with MB-25s and pulse-pistols and N-44s, then past a booth where a man would pray with you for a small fee. It was never-ending here, he knew. There was always someone willing to do something for money. Kimber stayed with him as he moved through the sea of people like a shark, set only on one goal.

They crossed Inkwell and left the Bazaar behind them. Two blocks left, Takashi told himself. And he'd only had to kill three people.

Cigarette smoke filled the air as he and Kimber passed a dance club called Dragon's Tears. The patrons stood outside and smoked, talking and laughing with each other. Takashi led Kimber around them and into the street for a brief stint, then they were back on the sidewalk. More bars and tattoo parlors and body-mod specialists and even a door that advertised bionic limbs at low prices.

He didn't wait for the crossing light at the next intersection, Cannon Street. He kept Kimber behind him as he stepped into the road, once again receiving honks and shouts and middle fingers. But he could now see his destination, and he wanted to get there as quickly as possible without attracting any undue attention. He noticed that while he had stopped the traffic, other pedestrians had taken advantage of the moment. Future Goths and Harajuku Girls and a group of cyberpunks all followed behind him, and the number of horns increased twofold.

The bars and clubs and various fronts passed by in a blur now. He didn't even look at them as he passed. He shouldered aside people. He stepped over a drunk. He moved into the street where necessary to get around large groups who had taken up the sidewalk. At length, he reached the final intersection, Dusseldorf Avenue. He took a left, bringing Kimber with him, and crossed the street between a stopped taxi and a Halperin Outlander. Then he counted three doors on his right. Where a fourth should have been was instead a narrow alley that led between two large buildings. It was filled with trash and refuse from the city. Takashi followed this alley halfway down, then knocked twice on an anonymous, rusted-out steel door. He waited exactly two seconds, then knocked twice more.

The door swung open, and a woman wearing green scrubs stepped aside to let him and the girl inside. The nurse, who looked only twenty-five or so, shut the door behind them. "The Surgeon is ready," she said. "Wait here."

"I've got a call to make," Takashi said to Kimber. He indicated a small waiting room in front of them, containing four chairs and a tiny table covered with ragged magazines. "Have a seat." He waited while she chose a seat at random and sat down. Then he touched one finger to the device in his ear. "It's me," he said after two rings. "The refugee is at the Surgeon's place. We're just waiting on him to get started."

"We've got you," said Thrash. "Sit tight and wait it out."

Takashi hung up the phone and dropped it into his jacket pocket. Then he sat down next to the refugee and picked up an ancient magazine. Flipping it open, he began to read.

~~~

Agent Ellis watched the Japanese man and the girl enter the building through the set of Nite-Specs held in his hands. When the door closed behind the two, he lowered the Nite-Specs and set them down on the ledge in front of him. From up here, on the fifteenth floor, he had needed the device to see the alley. And he needed the light-amp the device offered in order to pick out who was who. The alley had been crawling with people a few hours ago, but none had opened the door and entered the makeshift clinic.

Ellis stood back from the ledge. Behind him, Agents Holland and Graves stared into the heart of the city, their minds elsewhere. "Look alive, gentlemen," Ellis said. "Targets are in the building. Time to call the boss." He withdrew a smartphone from his jacket pocket and punched in a number. He waited two rings for the gruff voice to answer. "Yes?"

"It's Ellis, sir. The girl just went into the Surgeon's clinic. Should we take her now?"

"Negative. Let the Surgeon do the work. Take them both when they come out of there. The Jap is expendable, but the girl is to be brought back alive, understand? And get the implant. They want both this time. No mistakes."

"Yes, sir. I'll take care of it."

There was a click on the other end as the call was ended. Ellis slipped the phone back into his jacket, then pulled a small walkie-talkie from his belt. He brought it to his mouth and depressed the transmit button. "Team B, you still with us down there?"

A burst of static, followed by, "Still here, Lead."

"Targets are inside the building now. We'll keep an eye on it. When they exit, you take them. Kill the bodyguard, but the girl is to be kept alive, understand?"

"Roger, Lead. We're on it."

"Good. Stay alert. Shouldn't be too long." Ellis clipped the walkie-talkie to his belt and lifted the Nite-Specs from the ledge, bringing them to his eyes once more.

~~~

The hot water washed away the grime and the dirt and most of the garbage smell, but it couldn't wash away Spider's feelings. Even a man as hard as him. He felt terribly sad for the girl, Kimber. He knew that over half of the … refugees … never recovered from what they had gone through. It was merely the beginning of a lifelong hell, a trauma that led some to suicide, some to new-age religions, and some to prescription drugs. Still others sought counseling or psychiatric help. Some sought the comfort of others like themselves. That last one, that was what he was familiar with. He knew people who had connections with those groups. As he rinsed the shampoo from his hair for the second time, he wondered if that wasn't what God had in mind once the refugee got back.

His mind scolded him for using that word, refugee, because he knew what they were, yet he refused to use the proper term. Even now, as his mind wagged its mental finger at him, he still couldn't use the word. Or think it. Or even let it have space in his mind. If he did, he knew what the outcome would be: he would have to accept it. He would have to accept that what happened to these people was something he, and most of the world, could not explain. And it had been happening more and more in the last few years. He knew that because he saw the results as they were funneled down the line to their Surgeons.

He stuck his face under the hot spray, letting the water wash over him. He stuck his tongue out and took a mouthful, swishing it and spitting it out. The water had a vulgar taste to it, not unlike a child's sour candy. The filtration system must be acting up again. Built out of leftover parts by a man who once worked for Quartez, the system was prone to breakdowns and maintenance constantly. The only positive side was, when it did need to be fixed, it let you know by the sour taste of the water. He'd have to mention it to one of the tech monkeys and get somebody out here who could fix it. If not, then he'd take a whack at it himself. While computers were not his thing, basic engineering skills had been part of his upbringing in Brooklyn. The riots had devastated the city for months, and those inside had been on their own. Many people starved or froze to death during that time. But not Spider's family. His father had been an engineer with Hamza Electric, a company that sub-contracted to the city. His father had been able to repair and replace much of their damaged apartment. Their heat had been working while their neighbors froze. Spider wondered if he didn't get his hard heart from his father.

Spider gave his arm a sniff. The scent of garbage still lingered. He sighed and began to lather himself up for the third time.

The girl returned to his thoughts. Try as he might, he could not keep her out. The look that had been on her face when she first sat down in that chair only two or three feet in front of him. That was what did it, he supposed. He had seen the look on a hundred other faces, both male and female, but it had never done to him what it did on this night. There was something about her, something he couldn't put his finger on, that had led his mind to become … He stopped the train of thought in the middle of its tracks. He wasn't. There was no way. He was a businessman, a man who had few attachments. He was a man who did what he had to do in order to survive in this place.

But she wouldn't leave.

Her face remained at the forefront of his brain. Nothing seemed to make it go away. He tried everything. Even picturing the encounter he had with Bridgit earlier in the night didn't help. Kimber's face seemed to be permanently lodged in his head. He could picture the delicate curve of her chin, the angle of her tiny nose, the way her short blond hair fell in waves across her head, draping her face just so—

Spider shook his head, sending droplets of water flying across the shower stall. He reached forward and adjusted the water's temperature, feeling that familiar sting. The warmer water drove the thoughts from his head. He was grateful, but only for a few minutes. The thoughts returned as he lathered up his hair once more, trying to get the garbage stink out. He knew it was more than likely pointless. He had let the stink sit on him, and his irreplaceable suit, for far too long. Not his fault. He had business to take care of. But now, he wished he had done this as soon as he got to the club. Instead, he wasted the opportunity, and now he was probably going to smell like rotten garbage for the rest of the night and tomorrow as well.

He eyed the window ledge to his left, the place where his own bath supplies, as well as those of his two regular employees, rested. The window itself had been bricked over long before, the slightly brighter shade of red announcing the window's lost shape. Spider stared at the window's remains as the water cascaded down his back, drawing invisible lines across his old tattoos. The Japanese dragon that took up most of his back was a reminder of his time spent in Brooklyn and the parlor where he had gotten the tattoo done over the course of two weeks. That had been nearly six years after the riots and four years after Reconstruction began. He shook the memories from his head.

As he felt the water on his back, Spider finally gave up and let his mind wander. The girl floated through his head, as did Bridgit. The last week of his life: paying Mother, the prostitute on the corner of Desperation and Avantula, the job he had pulled only two days ago. But out of it all came the girl's face, her eyes bright and a smile on her face. He had not seen her smile, nor seen her eyes brighten, but he could imagine what they looked like, couldn't he? There was no law against that. He could imagine her any way he wanted to, but he didn't. He knew where his mind wanted to go, and that was where he drew the line. He wouldn't let it.

He stood under the shower for five more minutes, trying to think of nothing at all while he let the hot water wash over him. Then he switched off the water, reaching out of the shower stall for a nearby towel.

After the shower, he replaced his fallen Idio Nagata with another one of the designer's trademarks: the classic all-black. He liked the cut and he liked the fabric. It suited him, to coin a phrase. He finished getting dressed, then left the living quarters and headed out into the Hive.

Thrash had returned with dinner from a place down the street, and Spider tucked into his noodles with relish. It had been over twelve hours since he had last eaten. He wolfed the noodles down in under five minutes, then tossed the empty box into a nearby trashcan. "Where are they?" he asked, not caring who gave him the answer.

"They've been at the Surgeon's for the last twenty minutes," said Severen. "Nurses are prepping her now. Tak called in while you were washing that fucking stink off of you."

Spider made a note to stick a tack in Severen's chair the next time he went to take a leak, then turned his attention to Thrash. "Anything from God?"

"Quiet as a church mouse. Nothing doing so far."

"Good. I'm going to get a drink. If something changes—"

"Call you," Severen finished for him. "We know."

Spider left his team to it, climbing the spiral staircase to the door. Outside, he noticed that Finnegan had cleaned up the mess. All the blood and brain matter from Dauphine's pulse-pistol shots had disappeared. He hoped Finnegan enjoyed the drink.

Inside the club, Marisol followed closely behind him with his bottle of Chivas and two glasses. "Quartez is looking for you," she said. "She wants you to call her when you get here. Should I tell her you're at your table?"

Spider smiled and said, "Absolutely."

Marisol set his bottle down on his table and darted off. Spider sat down and poured himself a glass, then tipped it to the club and thought about how good it was to have people in here that were loyal to him, not Quartez. People like Marisol and Dauphine. Quartez was worried only about her bottom line. Spider had to make sure that bottom line included him as well. It was a constant struggle for power.

Spider took another sip of his drink as he heard a familiar melody come on over the club's sound system. He checked his watch and noted the time. Right on schedule. Busy as they all were backstage, the girls (and Quartez) knew that the twelve-thirty show was a huge draw for the club. Even now, Spider could see more people, Goths and cyberpunks and other citizens of the Red, moving closer to the stage and jockeying for position. Everyone wanted to see the show that made the club famous. Spider himself was indifferent. He enjoyed the show, just like everyone else, but he didn't feel the need to be in here at twelve-thirty every night to catch it.

As he watched, Quartez came out onto the stage, holding a wireless microphone in one hand. The crowd applauded her, and Quartez took in the admiration the same way he had seen her do many times before. She brought the mike to her mouth and began to speak. "Good evening, ladies and gentlemen," she said, even though everyone knew there were hardly any ladies in the club, and far less gentlemen. Everyone here was a hustler in their own way, whether it was drugs or guns or software or human beings or even time. "As you all know, we are world-famous for the show you are about to watch. Using the techniques taught to her by a Hindu man from the deepest parts of India, Dauphine will hypnotize all of you with her dance." Spider knew the show was nothing but mind-tricks, and he knew most of the audience was aware of that fact as well, but they all went along with the shared delusion that it wasn't an act, that Dauphine could really hypnotize them with her—

Quartez finished up. "And now, The Cat O' Nine Club proudly presents Dauphine and her boa!" The club exploded with applause and catcalls as Quartez left the stage and the club's lights dimmed. The melody increased in volume, and the curtains parted to let Dauphine, now dressed in only a blue lacey bra and panties, out onto the stage. Draped across her neck was a six-foot boa constrictor, its tongue lashing out to test the air.

Dauphine moved across the stage and danced with the serpent, using it to taunt and tease the audience. Whether or not she could actually hypnotize them with her act didn't seem to matter. The crowd was enthralled with her dance. Spider raised his glass to her and drank off the remainder of his Chivas. Dauphine flashed him a wink and continued with her routine.

Spider turned away from the stage and poured himself another glass. Before he could sip it, Quartez appeared in front of his table. Spider tipped his glass to her. "You wanted to see me?"

Quartez took the chair just in front of him, the same chair Kimber had been sitting in, and glared at him. "I just had a conversation with four Russian businessmen about you."

"Oh yeah?" He could barely keep the sarcasm from his voice. "You got some new clients looking for a good time tonight?"

Quartez shook her head. "Not even close. They were a goon squad, and a bit too obvious about it. They came in while you were busy with that abductee in the Hive."

Spider flinched without thought at her use of the word. He had been working to keep it out of his mind, to keep the word from gaining a foothold. But it seemed it was no use now. Quartez had put it right out there in the open. He tried to mentally push the word away, but it remained lodged inside his head. Instead, he ignored it for now. "What did they want?"

"I couldn't tell you. They asked to speak with you, and when I told them that you were busy at the moment, they up and left." She narrowed her eyes at him. "I don't need whatever heat this is, Spider. Not now, not when we're so close to a deal with Kobiyashi—"

Spider knew, just like everyone else did, why Quartez was pushing so hard with Kobiyashi Corporation. Bringing them in, treating them like kings in her own place, allowing them to have their pick of any of the girls, including Bridgit. He knew what her endgame was, and he didn't like it. And now, with her … accusations, he could no longer keep his disdain in check.

"Fuck your deal," he said, sipping his drink. "We all know why you're courting Kobiyashi. You want them to sell you Bots on the cheap to replace the girls here. Bots aren't alive and they don't complain, so you don't have to pay them. Pure profit on your part, Quartez. But let me ask you this: do you honestly think that's going to happen? You think all the girls in here are gonna lie down and let you replace them with nuts and bolts?" He shook his head. "Never gonna happen, so let that dream die, baby. You've replaced the greeters and most of the bartenders. That's as far as it'll go. Oh, you'll get a few Bots in here to supplement things. But you'll never replace these girls. And the reason is simple: they won't let you. You don't run this club, Quartez, it runs you, and you know it. So do yourself a favor and forget all that shit. Because your employees will leave you in that alley back there for Finnegan to clean up if you try to replace them." He pointed to the stage, where Dauphine was still dancing with her snake. The serpent wound its way up her leg and around her waist, just as she had trained it. "You think a Bot can replace that? Damn snake won't go anywhere near it. And Dauphine will never let you replace her with a Bot." He downed his drink and slammed the glass on the table. "That's the way it is."

"You son of a bitch," Quartez hissed. "You think you can talk to me like that?"

"I sure do. You forget that I'm not your employee, *Diana*. We have a mutually beneficial relationship. That dies the second these girls are on the street."

"So now you think you can dictate terms to me?"

"Did we sign a contract? Can you sue me if I decide to take my business, and my team, elsewhere? No, I don't think so. You need me just as much as I need you—"

"Not when there are Russians asking around about you in my club."

"I'll take care of that." He grinned at her. "You just take care of your bottom line, got it? Let me worry about the Russians."

"Easy for you to say. You don't have all this on the line." She swept a hand behind her at the club itself. "Anything happens to it, and we're both out on the street."

"You are. Not me."

"Arrogant little prick," she muttered in Japanese.

"Self-righteous bitch," Spider retorted, using Russian.

Quartez pushed back from the table and stood up. "You keep at this and Finnegan will be cleaning *you* up in that alley." This was in Spanish.

"Blow me." German.

"Asshole." French.

Spider switched to Portuguese, one language he knew Quartez did not speak. "You are an ignorant, filthy, inbred streetwalker turned whorehouse madam. You are no better than me." He flashed her a smile, then poured himself another drink. "Have a nice day."

Quartez stormed off, grunting to herself. This only made Spider's smile deepen. He was never sure, but he thought that maybe Quartez wanted to fuck him. How else could you explain the way she constantly harassed him? She'd never admit it, but there it was. He took a sip of his Chivas, then turned his attention back to the club.

Dauphine had just wrapped up her snake dance and was making her way backstage. The music gradually switched over to a heavier dance beat as Ellagarta, Vinyssa, and Renada strutted out, wearing their best smiles. Each was dressed as a different female superhero. Spider shook his head and turned away. This one could use a little work.

6

SPIDER'S PHONE RANG a few minutes later, as he was refilling his glass.

He fished it out of his jacket and turned away from the stage, bringing the phone to his ear. "Yeah?"

There was a moment of silence, then Spider could hear a hissing static sound that lasted for two or three seconds, then ceased. He smiled to himself. A call from a secure line like this usually meant work. The kind of work that actually paid.

"Is this Spider?" The voice was male, deep, with an edge of danger to it. The tone used was conspiratorial, something with which Spider was more than familiar.

"Yes it is. Who is this?"

The voice seemed hesitant, but it answered. "My name is Matsudo Ishi. I work for Flynn International Industries."

Now the voice had Spider's attention. He had received many calls like this over his long and storied career. It wasn't hard to determine, in his own mind, what the reason was behind the call. Spider knew he had a reputation among certain people. He also knew that corporate espionage was now punishable by a mandatory sentence of ten years in a federal prison. Since the system had become fully privatized back in '20, Spider feared what most denizens of the Red feared: incarceration in a privately run, for-profit prison. Once you went in, it was nearly impossible to get out. There was too much money to be made off your back.

"What can I do for you, Mr. Ishi?"

"I was told that you were the man to contact about this. I have need of your services."

"My services come with a price, Mr. Ishi. I hope you can afford me."

"Money is not an issue. But time is. I need the job done tonight."

Spider hesitated for a few moments. A job like this would pay him, and his staff, quite well. There was an inherent level of danger, but it did not dissuade him. He saw only the dollar signs that floated in front of his eyes. He knew they could all use the money. God had promised, in her own way, to pay him for this refugee job, but that was dubious at best. This was a guaranteed pay-day.

"Mr. Ishi, you are aware that what you're asking me to do is both highly illegal and very dangerous, correct?"

"I haven't even told you what the job is yet."

"People like yourself don't call me to make plans for coffee and pie. Like you said, I have a reputation. If you want the job done right and want it done tonight, it will not be cheap. Double the fee. Understand?"

"I told you, the money is no concern to me. Only the data concerns me."

"Understood. Do you know where the Cat O' Nine Club is, Mr. Ishi?"

"I do. Desperation Avenue, inside the Red District."

"Correct. How soon can you be here? I have other clients waiting." That was a lie, but it was one that had served him well in the past. Clients liked it when you were in-demand. It made them feel special.

"Ten minutes," Ishi answered.

"Okay. Once you're inside, management will take care of you. We have a process here that helps screen out unsavory people. Just follow your instructions and you'll get to me just fine. Understand?"

"Yes. I will be there soon." The call ended abruptly.

Spider stared at his phone for several seconds, then dropped the device into his jacket pocket. Flynn International, huh? Of course Spider knew the name. Just like nearly everyone else in the world, he used their products on a daily basis. Flynn Paper Products produced much of the material used for Prospect Parking Corporation's ticket machines. Flynn Toiletries, another subsidiary corporation, manufactured tooth paste and cotton swabs and hair brushes and even their own brand of deodorant. Harper-Flynn was a chain of grocery stores, bought several years ago through a hostile takeover. Flynn International was the umbrella beneath which all of the subsidiaries hid. It was a family business, once owned by the world-famous industrialist Algernon Flynn. The story went that after Algernon's death in a factory fire in Bangladesh, the man's son, Christopher, had inherited the controlling share in the company, but decided that he did not want it and sold his interest to his sister. Allegra Flynn had been running the company since then, despite being only twenty years old when she started. Under her reign, Flynn International had become more of a power player than they ever were before. The company's political donations spiked, funneling money to senators and representatives who could help the company maintain its influence. Allegra Flynn had been spotted by numerous gossip rags lunching with the president, as well as many senior House and Senate members. Flynn International's influence was the stuff of legend.

Of course Spider, like anyone else, knew the rumors about what had happened next. Christopher Flynn took his money and ran. He became obsessed with the supernatural, the weird, the off-kilter. He set out on a cross-country trip in an old Winnebago and began investigating strange phenomena. He ran a website called "strange-travels.com" where he logged everything he saw and investigated. Spider found himself smiling at this part, because as far as he was concerned, this was where it got interesting. According to legend, Chris Flynn had been married at the time, and his wife had travelled with him in the Winnebago, investigating with him. His wife's name? Elizabeth Wilder. He had been married to God.

Spider had never spoken about the rumors with God herself, but he figured that, much like God's reputation, there had to be at least fifty percent truth to the tale. But that was where the story ended. Christopher Flynn had been killed in a motel fire just outside Roswell, New Mexico about four years ago. No one knew the details of how God had escaped the fire, or even if she had been there at the time. There was some debate among conspiracy theorists as to whether or not Chris Flynn was actually dead, but as far as anyone could prove, he had burned up in that motel four years ago.

Spider checked his watch, noting the time, and stood up. He buttoned his jacket and walked through the VIP area to his door, punching in the code without giving it any thought. He stepped outside into the Red, his eyes darting left and scanning the four, no, five girls standing beneath the club's spotlights. Smoke drifted between the girls as he picked out Dauphine, Madrid, Mitsuko, Ariana, and … that was the new girl, Molly. He didn't know what her stage name was, or even if she had chosen one, but he had briefly entered the room when Quartez had been interviewing the girl.

"Hey, Spider." Dauphine.

Spider threw up one hand in a wave. "Ladies," he said.

Then he was at the other door, and he punched in the second code. The door popped open and Spider crossed the threshold into the Hive. He made sure the door locked behind him, then he descended the stairs, where he found Thrash and Severen behind their terminals. Thrash seemed to be keeping an eye on Takashi, while Severen was busy shooting his way through the newest version of *Galdar's Castle*.

"Eyes up," Spider said as he passed between the terminals. He turned to face them. "We have work."

Severen dropped the game controller and sat up. Thrash merely turned her gaze to him, focused. "What kind of work?" she asked.

"Bust and bail. I just got a call from a gentleman who works for Flynn International. He needs us to steal some data. He didn't go into much more detail than that."

"Galvatronix is Flynn's biggest competitor," said Severen.

"Only for electronics," Thrash said. "Flynn has cornered the market on almost everything else."

"Except for defense contracts. Galva has more DoD projects behind their firewalls than Flynn could ever hope for."

Thrash waved a hand. "Nothing but drone specs and the latest facial-recognition software—"

"—and kill codes for cell phones," Severen added.

"Give me a break," Thrash muttered.

"Is that it, boss? Are we cracking Galva tonight?" Severen asked.

"Unknown." Spider checked his watch. "He'll be here in eight and a half minutes. When he does, I'll get the low down and you two will take care of business." He pointed to Thrash. "Make sure you keep an eye on Tak and the girl." She nodded. Spider continued. "I'll be in the club. Expect me shortly. I'll be able to share more then. Hopefully this will be a walk in the park for you two. We could use the money."

"No shit, boss," said Severen.

Spider turned and walked back to the stairs without a word. He left the Hive behind him and stepped outside.

The girls were now on his right. Dauphine and the new girl had gone inside, but the others remained. Spider could see the pulse-pistols tucked into the waistbands of their tiny skirts. He smiled to himself as he crossed the catwalk to the other door, punching in his code and swinging the door open.

Down-tempo music hit his ears, and he glanced at the stage. Two girls he couldn't immediately identify were swaying back and forth while a third, who looked like Briyanna, slowly stripped between them. Spider ignored the display and made his way to the bar, where Bridgit was currently mixing drinks for a group of Middle Eastern businessmen who had made their home in the back corner of the VIP area with several of the girls. She flashed him a smile as she finished with the drinks, then handed them off to Marisol, who brought the drinks to the table. Spider turned away when she arrived there. He knew what would happen. If it got out of hand, Bridgit would take care of it. If not, then he'd do it himself.

"What can I get you, Spider?" Bridgit asked him, her smoky voice tingling his spine.

"Get the word out," he replied. "I've got a client coming around in about—" He checked his watch. "Seven minutes. Let Quartez know, and make sure the guy is taken care of. Have one of the girls escort him up here."

"Sure you don't want a drink?" She teased him with her words, the twinkle in her eye telling him she was looking for round two.

He shook his head. "Not right now. Business first." He pointed to his table. "Send Marisol around with my bottle and two glasses when she's finished."

"No problem."

Spider turned and made his way to his table, sitting down in his customary seat. He slid the pulse-pistol out of its holster and flicked the safety off, laying the weapon on his thigh. With Takashi out on a job, security was left to him. Not that he couldn't handle it. Having Tak around just made him feel better. The Japanese man was worth every penny that his services cost. And Spider trusted him, which was a hard thing to come by around the Red.

He checked his watch. Four minutes.

Marisol came around with his bottle and the glasses. He smiled at her and slipped her a twenty. "For the trouble they cause you," he said, and indicated the group in the corner.

Marisol returned his smile. "Thanks, Spider. You're a peach."

"No I'm not. Back to work."

Marisol disappeared behind the bar.

Spider poured himself a drink and took a sip. The bottle was getting low tonight. Almost time for a new one. He smiled to himself; free liquor was another perk of working here. Quartez's client base more than made up for any losses that his drinking might have incurred.

Exactly three and a half minutes later, Dauphine appeared at the top of the stairs with a middle-aged Japanese man in tow. The man wore a very expensive brown suit and carried a silver briefcase. Spider could see the gleam of corneal implants in the man's eyes. And why not? In his native country, the technology wasn't illegal like it was here. *Only in America*, thought Spider.

Dauphine led the man to Spider's table. Spider watched the man to see how he reacted to the club, but the man gave no outward indication that he cared about the meeting place. Dauphine smiled at Spider as she approached. "Hi, Spider," she said. "This man is here to see you."

Dauphine

"Thanks, doll." Dauphine turned and walked off towards the stairs, but one of the Middle Eastern businessmen stopped her before she could get very far. She should've expected it after the snake dance.

Matsudo Ishi was a fastidious-looking man. His close-cropped hair and his manicured nails and his suit gave the appearance of a successful businessman, but the fact that he had contacted Spider about a job meant that while he may be successful, he was certainly less than respectable. But Spider had learned that in his line of work, respectability was a hard trait to come by. "Thank you for seeing me," Ishi said, as he sat down in the chair opposite Spider.

Spider poured a generous amount of Chivas into the second glass, sliding it across the table. "How can I help you, Mr. Ishi?"

"I need to … recover certain data. It has to be done in the next hour. I have a plane to catch."

"Can you be a little more specific?"

The man set his briefcase down next to him. He seemed to lean closer. "I was recently fired by Allegra Flynn herself. You see, I was an executive vice president within the company. I had spent many years working my way up to that position. I fought to get it. And then …" He stopped, shaking his head. "Corporate politics are not what they used to be. Before … things were different. Now, with the level of corporate freedom that your country enjoys, there is very little policing done, internally or externally. And certain practices are being allowed to continue, despite the fact that they are highly illegal. Kidnapping, for example. Human experimentation. That sort of thing." He took a breath. "I am taking the data that

I need from the Flynn International mainframe before I leave your country and return home."

"What kind of data are we talking about here?"

"You don't need to know that. All you need to know is that I have your payment." He pointed to the briefcase. "Inside, you will find the money and instructions to get you inside the corporate mainframe. Once you have the data in hand, erase the original file and crash the server. Based on your reputation, this should be no problem for a man like yourself."

Spider sipped his drink, considering the proposition. Breaking into a corporate server was more than just illegal, it was dangerous. Flynn International had a bad reputation for vendettas. The upside was, his team was very good at what they did. There was a good chance they could get in and out with time to spare. Spider set the glass down in front of him. "I think I can help you, Mr. Ishi." He put on a smile. "Wait here."

The man shook his head. "I need to see the data for myself."

"And you will. Once I have it in my hand. No one sees the operation, understand? It's for your safety as well as mine." He pointed to the stage. "Enjoy the show for the next little bit. I'll be back soon." He stood up and buttoned his jacket. When he reached for the briefcase, Ishi slid it away with one foot. "You'll get the instructions now. But the payment stays with me until I see the data."

Spider shrugged. "If that's how you want to do it. Makes no difference to me." He stepped aside as Ishi lifted the briefcase onto the table and snapped the latches open. Inside, Spider could see stacks of hundred dollar bills, covered by several sheets of paper. Ishi lifted these sheets out of the case, then snapped it closed. He handed the sheets of paper to Spider and said, "Good luck."

"Won't need it," Spider said as he took the sheets. He signaled Marisol behind the bar. "Marisol here will take care of you, Mr. Ishi. Have a few drinks and enjoy yourself."

Marisol planted herself in the Japanese man's lap as Spider headed for the door.

Once he was back in the Hive, he gave Thrash and Severen a brief overview of the meeting, then told Thrash that he wanted an ID check run on the man immediately. Thrash complied, and swung one of the club's many cameras around to Spider's table. She focused the camera and cleaned up the image as best she could, then ran that image through her own programs. In seconds, she had gotten a response: he was who he said he was.

"So he's stealing from his own company?" Thrash asked. "That's a little odd. Did he say anything else? Maybe he's got a buyer lined up over there."

Spider shook his head. "Nothing else. Just that he needed the data in an hour. So get to it, you two."

Thrash cracked her knuckles. "No sweat, boss. This is practice."

"Yeah," Severen agreed, "Give us something harder next time."

Spider smiled to himself as he sat down on the ratty sofa and began the wait.

Thrash cued up some music, which would keep him from falling asleep. Not that he was tired. It was the sofa's fault. He had no idea where the piece of furniture had come from, but one day, it had simply appeared here. He didn't ask his tech monkeys who it belonged to or how it got here. He simply went with it. But the thing was comfortable, that's for sure. He had spent many nights catching a few hours of needed rest on it. He had even had a few refugees spend the night on it when things were tough.

He wasn't worried about his people running into trouble. They were professionals, and had been doing this in one capacity or another since they were children. The ease with which they commanded technology in general and computers in particular astounded him. He would never let them know it, that might undermine his authority, but he felt it nonetheless. They could do so much from this very room, never leaving the Hive. Thrash could hack banks and transfer millions. Severen could hack car manufacturers and have a brand-new cherry-red Bravaddo delivered here in a few hours. The sheer power that Spider wielded from this room frightened even him sometimes.

"We're in," Thrash announced. "We've picked up the trail."

"Somebody buried this, boss," said Severen. "It's behind more security than I've seen on a corporate network in a long time."

"This is big time," said Thrash. "We've got a doozy here, boss."

"Get it done," Spider said. "In and out. Don't fuck around."

Thrash grunted. "If we don't decrypt it, we'll have no idea what it is we're down-loading."

"The client doesn't want us to know, remember?" Spider tried to keep the irritation out of his voice. "Don't worry about it. Get it and get out."

"They've got some serious muscle behind this," Severen threw in. "I mean, this system was designed by somebody who really knew what they were doing. The programming—"

"Jerk off to it later," Spider said. "Do your job."

"Okay, okay."

Spider checked his watch. Plenty of time.

"Shit," said Severen. "Somebody knows we're here."

"Hurry this along then."

"We've got a tail," Thrash announced. "Somebody's backtracing us."

Spider stood up and moved closer to the computer banks. "If you can't get it, drop out and start over in a few minutes. We've got the time."

"They'll lock it down," Thrash retorted. "If they're coming after us this hard, they'll kick us out and kill the file. And we won't get paid."

Spider found his arms crossing themselves without his knowledge, his usual reaction at times like this. "How long on the backtrace?"

"Fifty six seconds," Severen answered. "I can run them through some phony IPs and—"

"Do it. Pull out all the stops. Everything you've got."

Severen began to type furiously, and Thrash wasn't far behind. Spider tried not to let the doubt creep in, but it was there. This was something that they hadn't encountered before. But then again, they had never hacked the Flynn International mainframe. It hadn't occurred to him that this might happen. He silently scolded himself for not considering the possibility. He'd let the money blind him to the danger. *Stupid*, he thought. And it wasn't the first time.

"I found it," said Thrash. "Starting the download now."

Spider pointed to his other tech. "Back her up. And slow down that fucking backtrace."

"Working on it, boss."

"Twenty percent," said Thrash. "Thirty."

Spider tried to ignore the beads of sweat that popped up on his forehead. If the backtrace found them, the whole Hive was over and down with. He'd have to burn the place down and salt the earth to get away clean. There wasn't enough time for that, not nearly enough.

"Sixty percent, boss."

He tried to think about the money. That usually helped. But this time, it did not. The money meant shit if he had to blow town. Despite his outward appearance, he liked it here. It was a good place to do business. He didn't want to leave. He had a good thing going.

"Almost there, boss. Eighty percent."

"How's that backtrace?"

"They're getting closer, boss. I'm throwing everything I have at them, but it's not slowing them down like I thought it would. They've got somebody really good on the other side."

"Ninety percent, boss." Another five seconds. "That's it."

"Kill the file, crash the server, and get the hell out." He waved his hand in the air as Thrash typed furiously on her keyboard. Then she grinned, leaning back and kicking her feet up on the console. "It's done. Nothing to it, big cheese. All in a day's work."

"Get your feet off the hardware," Spider snapped. "Give me the drive."

Thrash stuck her tongue out at him, then handed him a small thumb drive. "You don't have to be so mean, boss."

Spider shook his head. "That was a close one, you two. Do better next time."

"Yes sir!" Severen shouted, and snapped off an exaggerated salute.

Spider climbed the stairs to the door and threw it open. A breeze brought the smells of the Red to his nose, filled now with more auto exhaust than before. The tall buildings sometimes trapped the clouds of pollution between them. He looked around and saw a haze around the neon on Desperation Avenue. Fucking Orange District smog. He shook his head and let the door close behind him. The locks engaged, and Spider crossed the catwalk to the second door. He put the code in and opened it.

There was a heavier dance beat playing now. Spider could feel it in his bones as it shook the club. He checked the stage. Dauphine was back up, now paired with Meridian and Ellegarta, who was filling in for Marisol. Spider turned his eyes to the table he called his own, and saw that Mr. Ishi was still there, now surrounded by Marisol, Molly the new girl, as well as Ariana, Bella, and Satoshi. Behind the bar, Bridgit tossed him a glance as he made his way to the table.

"Mr. Ishi," Spider said, laying a hand on the man's shoulder. He turned his smile to the girls gathered around the table. "Ladies, I need a minute with this gentleman, if you don't mind."

The girls laughed and gathered their clothes, heading for the stairs. Satoshi leaned in and whispered in Spider's ear. "Don't be so upscale, Spider. It's why we love you." Then she joined the other girls and departed down the stairs.

Spider took his seat, still wearing the smile. "Enjoying yourself?"

Ishi wore a smile a mile wide. "I had no idea that this club was so ... is naughty the right word?"

Spider nodded. "Indeed it is." He slid the thumb drive across the table. "Your data. Encrypted, of course, but I figure that you're a man who can take care of that sort of thing."

Ishi nodded. "I can."

"Good. And the money?"

Ishi lifted the briefcase and slid it across the table to Spider. "Double your usual fee, as you specified."

Spider opened the case and checked the bills, then did a quick calculation. It was all there. He snapped the case closed and tucked it behind his chair, then stood up. "Then that's it. Nice doing business with you, Mr. Ishi. Come back anytime."

The Japanese man stood as well, then inclined his head. "You live up to your reputation. Thank you."

"Think nothing of it. Enjoy your flight."

"I will." The man turned and walked off into the club, heading for the stairs.

Spider waited until Ishi was gone before he lifted the case and carried it with him into the Hive. His tech monkeys were overjoyed to get paid for their work with actual money instead of promises. He listened to them talk of extravagant meals and new clothes and better computers until he could stand it no longer. He checked his watch. Kimber's operation should be nearly finished. Tak should be checking in soon.

"I'm going for a drink," he said. "Call me when Tak checks in and give me an update. When he gets back, send him up with the girl."

"You got it, boss," said Severen.

7

THE NEXT FIFTEEN minutes passed quickly. There were no more visits from Russian businessmen or potential clients, nor did Quartez return to bother him again. Spider watched the acts on the stage with a detached eye, one that was no longer excited by the perversions the girls performed on each other. He had seen it all before. He checked his watch only once during that time.

His phone rang at eight minutes before two. He knew what the call was. "Takashi and the girl are leaving the Surgeon's place now," Thrash told him. "He's got the implant with him."

"Good. Call me if there's a problem."

"Will do, boss."

Spider slid the phone back into his jacket and reached for his drink. The glass was inches from his hand when it was picked up by Bridgit. She downed the Chivas and set the glass on the table, eyeing him. "I'm off at five," she said. "Wanna head back to my place for the night?"

Spider grinned at her. "How can I say no to an offer like that?"

Then his phone rang again.

"Shit." He reached into his jacket and yanked the phone out, bringing it to his ear. "What is it?"

"Boss, we got a problem." It was Severen.

"No shit."

"Tak's got a tail."

"I'm on the way." Spider ended the call and dropped the phone into his jacket. He stood up. "Put the girls on full alert," he told Bridgit. "We've got incoming."

Bridgit didn't wait to hear another word. She was on her feet in seconds, running towards the stairs. Behind the bar, Marisol didn't need to see or hear anything other than that. She reached below the cedar for a pulse-pistol and made sure it was loaded. Spider jogged across the VIP area to his door, punching in the code as fast as he could. Outside, he could see Janessa and Damascus smoking under one of the lights. He whistled to get their attention, then cupped his hands around his mouth as he jogged to the other door. "Get inside! Red alert!" The two pitched their cigarettes and ran for the club's back door. As he punched in the second code, he could hear the bolts being thrown on the door below him. Good. Until he had a handle on the situation, it was better to err on the side of caution. The last thing he wanted was for one or more of these girls, people who were just doing their jobs, to be hurt because of him. The door beeped at him as it accepted the code, then he threw it open and stepped into the Hive.

~~~

Takashi closed the magazine, an old copy of *Spangler's Muscle Cars*, and tossed it onto the degraded coffee table as the nurse in the green scrubs came through a door and into the waiting room. His eyes met hers, and she smiled at him. "Everything went as planned," the nurse said. "Surgeon's sewing her up right now. He's got the implant."

"Very good," said Takashi. "Send her out when you're finished."

The nurse gave him a nod and turned on her heel, disappearing through the door once more.

Takashi took out his smartphone and dialed a number. Thrash picked up after two rings. "Yeah?"

"It's Tak. She's out of surgery. Being sewn up right now. We'll be leaving in five minutes."

"Copy that."

"Where's the boss?"

"Drinking at his table, more than likely."

"Tell him I called."

"Done."

Takashi hung up the phone and dropped it into his jacket pocket. He stood up and adjusted his tie. His right hand pulled the pulse-pistol and checked it for what seemed like the hundredth time. Full mag, safety off. He holstered it and buttoned his jacket.

Moments later, the same nurse led Kimber out of the door and into the lobby. She wore a white bandage around her left forearm, spotted with small drops of blood. Aside from that, she looked the same as she did before. No, that was wrong. Takashi could see something in her eyes, some change that indicated she was ... was that freedom? A sense of satisfaction? He couldn't tell, but something was there. Something had changed.

The nurse handed Takashi a plastic tube. Inside was a sliver of metal no bigger than a microchip. It had no markings. There were spots of blood inside the container and on the implant itself. Takashi dropped it into his pocket. Spider had told him to hold onto it because God wanted it.

He thanked the nurse and told her that payment would arrive in the morning, the same as it always did. He or Spider would personally carry it here. That was how it was always done. The nurse told him she was just doing her job, but accepted his thanks with humble appreciation. Takashi led Kimber to the door and gently eased it open.

~~~

Agent Ellis unclipped the walkie-talkie with one hand as he watched the Jap and the girl through the Nite-Specs. He spoke into it. "Team B, this is Lead. They're out. Move in and take them."

"Roger," came the whispered reply.

Ellis pocketed the walkie this time, not taking his eyes off the scene below him. He wanted to make sure. The boss had told him not to screw this one up, and he planned to adhere to that.

~~~

Noise and light suddenly filled Takashi's head as he stepped out of the Surgeon's place. Even here, in the back alleys of the Red District, the city's presence was still felt. Neon filtered in from high above and the street to his left, bringing with it the sounds of the city. Kimber exited behind him, staying as close as she could. Takashi let the door close behind him, then turned one eye to the girl. "Stay close to me," he said. "We're not out of the woods yet."

She nodded, but didn't speak. Her lack of words allowed him to hear the shifting of garbage and junk in the back of the alley. His eyes found the source of the sound. Two pale men were moving up the alley at a pace that set his hair on end. The meager light allowed him to see the off-the-rack suits the two pale men wore, and the single ear bud each had in his right ear. *Shit*, he thought. The suits and the ear buds told him all he needed to know.

Men in Black

Takashi shoved Kimber against the door with his left hand, then spun towards the men and drew his pulse-pistol. The first man already had a gun in his hand, but Takashi was faster. Before the first man could raise the weapon, Takashi fired a burst from the pulse-pistol, dropping him. The second man reached for his own weapon, and a second burst put him down just a few feet from the first body.

Takashi touched a finger to his ear piece. While it dialed the Hive, he helped Kimber to her feet. The girl didn't question his actions like he thought she would. Takashi had been trained not to fight with the protectee around. Stray bullets could end the job before it truly started. Now, he took Kimber by the hand as the phone continued to dial and began to lead her down the alley towards the two bodies.

Severen answered on the fourth ring. "That you, Tak?"

"It is. I've got a tail."

"Sit-rep." Severen was all business now.

"Two men came at us as we were leaving the Surgeon's place. Plain suits and ear buds. White as ghosts. Hold one. I'm going to make an ID." He reached the bodies and indicated with one hand that Kimber should remain still and not leave that spot. She did as ordered. Takashi went down on one knee and began to rummage through the first body's pockets. He found a key-fob remote for a late-model Halperin Hyperion, probably a rental, as well as a pack of American cigarettes, a lighter, two hundred dollars in cash (which he pocketed), and a wallet. The ID and badge within told Takashi that he had just killed two FBI agents. He repeated the process on the second body. No cash, no keys, and no cigarettes. This one simply had the same leather bi-fold with a badge and ID card tucked inside. Takashi tossed the wallet aside. "Both have federal IDs, but they're not as convincing as they should be. Obvious forgeries."

"Do we have mibs?" Severen asked, his voice carrying a bit of static across the line.

"Looks like it. No way these guys are feds. Not with these IDs."

"You know the protocol. Get some pictures on your phone and send them our way, then get your ass back here as soon as you can. I'll get the boss down here."

"Roger that." Takashi pushed the device's single button, and the call was ended. He gave Kimber a look and said, "Don't move." Then he took his phone from a pocket and switched on the camera. He snapped several pictures of both men's faces, then turned off the camera and began punching keys furiously. When he was finished, he slid the phone back into his pocket. He stood up and took Kimber by the arm. "Come on," he said. "We can't stay here."

She didn't ask questions. She simply followed him as he moved closer to the mouth of the alley. Then that feeling crept up his neck, setting the hairs on end. He grabbed Kimber and shoved her to the ground just as three bullets ricocheted off the wall where his own head had just been. Somebody wanted him dead to get to the girl. Why they wanted her, he could only begin to guess.

Takashi spun around and fired towards the rear of the alley. He emptied the magazine just to be sure, then popped the empty out and let it fall to the ground. He grabbed Kimber by her wrist and dragged her out of the alley behind him, leaving behind shouts and a single burst of gunfire.

They burst onto Dusseldorf Avenue in the middle of a traffic jam. Cabbies screamed at motorists and motorists screamed at pedestrians. Takashi took a few seconds to reload the pulse-pistol. He grabbed Kimber and dragged her with him across the street, weaving between cabs and cars and avoiding pedestrians. It wasn't until Takashi saw a man's head explode beside him and heard the burst of gunfire that he ducked, bringing Kimber with him, and ran flat-out for Desperation Avenue.

~~~

Spider threw open the door and slammed it behind him, shouting even as he came down the spiral stairs. "Talk to me! What the hell's going on?"

Thrash answered him first. "Tak's got heat on him. Taking fire now." She punched several keys, and the large screen lit up with fuzzy camera images of Desperation Avenue. "He just crossed Dusseldorf to Desperation."

"Is the girl still with him?"

Thrash nodded. "He's got her."

"What the hell happened?"

Severen took over while Thrash tapped at her keyboard and held one hand to her left ear. "He spotted them as he and the girl came out of the Surgeon's. Two men, wearing cheap suits and ear buds and looking pale as ghosts." Severen shook his head. "Something's not right, boss. Tak thinks they might be mibs."

Shit, Spider thought. *Mib* was a general term for … well, Spider knew what it was for. And if he thought about it, he'd have to admit, once more, that it was all true. *Mib* was colloquial slang for Men In Black. Spider knew the group existed. They had menaced several of his refugees before, according to the refugees' own accounts. They showed up and intimidated witnesses to … strange phenomena. They worked to discredit the witnesses who refused to remain quiet. Legend had it that the mibs were part of some top-secret Air Force program. Since no one had ever spoken to one without disappearing, it was hard to determine the truth. But they were here, and it seemed like they wanted the girl. For what, he had no idea.

"Pull him up on a map. Put it on the big guy. Split it between the map and the District cameras. And get him back on the phone."

Thrash punched keys until a satellite map of the Red District appeared on the large screen. Within it, Spider could see a flashing red dot. That dot was Takashi's GPS. Hopefully the girl was still with him. Keys were tapped behind him, and the screen suddenly split in two. One side was the map with Tak's dot, and the other was filled with smaller images of grainy black and white street views. Spider followed the dot as it moved down Desperation Avenue.

"Got him, boss," said Thrash. She tossed Spider a wireless headset, and he slid it on with ease.

"Tak, this is Spider. What's up?"

The reply was instant. "Two down in the alley off Dusseldorf. Unknown number following me now. Sent you pictures of the two dead guys."

Spider snapped his fingers at Thrash. "Pictures. Now."

Thrash nodded, then began to type on her keyboard. Spider turned away to let her work. "Tak? Cross Cannon and duck into Dragon's Tears on your right." Spider folded his arms. "Yumi is doing a concert there tonight. Try and lose them in the crowd inside."

"Roger." Takashi did not ask questions. He simply did as ordered.

Spider watched the dot deviate from its course, then it moved into a large building.

Thrash spoke up behind him. "I got nothing on these guys, boss. Maybe it's that white makeup they're wearing or maybe—"

"They're not in the system anymore," Spider finished for her. "They've been wiped. They don't exist." He shook his head. "Jesus Christ on a bicycle drinking whiskey. We've got real mibs here."

Thrash didn't say a word and neither did Severen.

~~~

Team B was down. Of that, Agent Ellis was sure. He had seen the Jap hit them both with some kind of jazz, probably a pulse-pistol from the sound of it. He hadn't stuck around to see the rest. He had ordered Holland and Graves down the stairs after the two, and he had followed behind them. Graves was the only one carrying anything heavier than a handgun for this mission, a FM-240 submachine gun. There didn't seem to be any reason for it on a simple grab mission, or so he had thought. Now, he wished he had something more than the SH15 in his hip holster.

The pursuit took them onto Dusseldorf Avenue, where the two were just reaching the other side of the street. He drew his own weapon and fired, just missing the Jap and splattering the brains of some junkie onto the sidewalk. Not that he cared. He had a job to do.

Ellis crossed the street with the other two agents close behind him.

~~~

Takashi ducked and dodged between groups of pedestrians, trying to keep out of sight. He knew the mibs would have no problem firing into the crowd if they spotted him. The evidence was still splattered across the left arm of his suit. Behind him, screams and shouts filled the air as the mibs made it onto Desperation Avenue. He could hear Japanese and German curses, then he heard the blast of a large-caliber handgun behind him, followed by a gargling scream.

Cannon Street was only fifty yards away now, if he could only make it through these crowds.

Cyberpunks spilled out of a bar to his right, and he had to shoulder a few of them aside as he made his way past. A few shoved him in return, but he was gone before any real trouble could start. *Good*, he thought, *maybe they'll slow the mibs down long enough to get into the club.* There was another blast of gunfire, followed by what sounded like the beginning of a brawl. More gunshots filled the air, and the people around him began to scramble off the street, finding cover wherever they could. Gun battles weren't uncommon here, and most people had survived at least one or two already.

The sidewalk cleared in seconds, giving him an open path to Cannon Street. He tightened his grip on Kimber and began to run faster, nearly dragging her behind him.

The mibs behind him were gaining, he knew it without having to look. The crowd had slowed him down more than he anticipated. Not that it mattered. If they had a shot, they'd take it. "Listen to me," Tak began, "if something happens to me, you take this gun and you run, understand? Straight down the street until you get back to the club."

Kimber nodded, her eyes filled with panic.

Another burst of gunfire. Takashi could feel the rounds pierce the air above his head. Kimber issued a scream, but much shorter and less panicky than Takashi would've suspected. Then they were hitting the intersection, and Takashi didn't bother to stop.

He dove off the curb in front of a JR Cab. The Bot driver's smile never left his face as he slammed the cab's brakes, just missing Takashi's shins. Then the Japanese man and his temporary ward were across, only yards from the entrance to Dragon's Tears.

The JR Cab moved forward into the street, then Takashi could hear another burst of gunfire. The Bot driver disintegrated in a spray of circuitry and coolant, splashing the cab's interior. Takashi turned and fired his own weapon as the three mibs climbed over the cab. He didn't hit any of them, but the burst caused them to drop behind the cab, buying him precious seconds.

~~~

Ellis and Graves dropped behind the taxi, their feet crunching diodes and circuitry from the destroyed Driver-Bot. Holland raised his weapon first to return fire, but saw immediately that there were too many people. The first shot would cause the Jap and the girl to duck away and bury themselves in the crowd.

Ellis raised his head and peeked over the cab's hood. He could just make out the Jap and the girl, heading towards a club several yards away. He turned to Agent Graves and said, "They're heading for the club. Take the back alley and cut them off. Remember: keep the girl alive."

Graves nodded and took off without a word, moving towards a small alley that ran behind the buildings and businesses on the right. He disappeared into the darkness, making no sound.

Ellis and Holland made their way over the cab and down the street. They could trap him and the girl inside the club, Ellis told himself. It would be simple. The crowd would work for him, not the Jap. The amount of bodies squeezed into the space would keep the Jap and the girl from moving through the club too fast.

Ellis drew his weapon as he and Holland approached the club.

~~~

The club's entrance was packed with 'punks and Future Goths and circuiters. A doorman stood to one side, and Takashi easily dodged around him. When he began to protest, Takashi pointed the pulse-pistol at him, and the man put his hands up. Takashi turned away and began to hustle the girl through the lobby and into the club proper.

A sleazy Japanese pop song suddenly filled his ears as Takashi pushed the club's doors open. Out of the corner of his right eye, he could see Yumi on the stage, holding a microphone in her hand while a DJ spun records behind her. The layer of bullet-proof glass between Yumi and the audience, in addition to the heavily-armed guards on either side of the stage, was a testament to the singer's popularity and infamy. Takashi immediately began to think of ways he could use these things to his advantage.

Yumi

The dance floor was filled with the Red's most colorful citizens, all dressed in their various finery. 'Punks and Goths and circuiters and dope-heads and info-junkies surrounded him, all here because Yumi was the most popular thing to ever hit the Red. The club was nearly filled to capacity, both a good and bad thing. It would slow the mibs down when they hit the door, but it would slow him down too.

Takashi yanked Kimber past a group of dancing surgery-junkies who were there to show off their scars. "We're in, boss." He had left the phone device on while he moved down the street.

Takashi felt a certain reassurance at the sound of his boss' voice. "Go out the back to the alley and follow it out to International Street. I've got a plan. It's a shitty plan, but it might work."

"Roger."

"You've got one coming down the alley to the back so hurry it up. No telling how many of them are loose out there."

Takashi didn't answer. Instead, he shoved aside a cyberpunk with dangling plastic tubes for hair and dragged Kimber across the dance floor. "Behind us!" she shouted, just managing to be heard over the music and noise of the crowd. Takashi turned, then shoved Kimber to the floor as he sighted his pulse-pistol on one of the mibs. The crowd surged forward as Yumi's song hit its crescendo, blocking his shot. But the mib had no shot, either. He could shoot indiscriminately into the crowd and risk Yumi's bodyguards blowing him away, or he could wait.

Takashi ducked and lifted Kimber to her feet without a word. This time, he had no trouble with her. In fact, she was getting ahead of him. "Slow down!" he shouted, and she dropped back to his side.

The crowd began to thin as the back door came into sight. Then it was thrown open and a third mib stepped into the club, brandishing a FM-240 submachine gun in his hands. Takashi had no choice. He used his right hand to sweep the gun's barrel to the side, then struck the mib in the throat with an open fist. The mib made choking sounds as his eyes widened. Takashi hit him in the solar-plexus and the mib doubled over. Takashi gave him a knee to the nose, dropping the mib to the floor. Takashi raised his pulse-pistol, took aim, and fired, putting four holes into the mib's chest in less than a second. The mib died instantly as the club-goers around the scene began to scream at the sound of the gunfire. Yumi's song immediately stopped and the crowd began to duck and cover. Not an unusual Wednesday night in the Red, to be sure.

Behind them, the thinning crowd was a boon for the remaining mibs. They raised their weapons and began to fire.

Takashi and Kimber reached the door as the gunfire began.

The mib closest to the stage went down in a hail of bullets, but his friend wasn't so slow. The bodyguard did not fire a second time. His brains were splattered against the bullet-proof glass, eliciting a scream from the departing Yumi, hustled away by the other bodyguards.

The remaining mib took aim, but Takashi was already shoving Kimber through the door and following behind her.

The alley was filled with refuse, but Takashi and Kimber picked their way through. "In the alley, boss," Takashi said. "Where to?"

"Get to International and take it down one block to Inkwell."

"Then what?"

"Call me."

Takashi didn't say another word. He kicked aside a pile of trash and picked up the pace.

~~~

Graves and Holland were dead. Ellis left their bodies in the club as he moved to the back door, no thought given whatsoever to the two men who had accompanied him on this mission. They were simply collateral damage that would be cleaned up at a later date. He had an objective, a goal. That was all that mattered. Dead colleagues could be taken care of.

He pushed his way through the screaming crowds, shoving aside circuiters and junkies and J-Pop freaks as he moved to the back door. A bouncer stopped him with an arm the size of a redwood trunk as he got closer. This problem was solved with two rounds to the bouncer's head. The shots sent the remaining club-goers screaming and running for the exits, pushing and shoving to be first out the door. Not one of them made a move for the back door.

Ellis let his gun lead the way out the door, but the alley was already empty. There were only a few places the Jap could run to from here. Agent Ellis decided on the left side of the alley, and began to run.

~~~

"What's the plan, boss?" Severen asked.

Spider waved a hand. "Never mind that. Bring up some shots of International Street." This road, Spider knew, ran parallel to Desperation through most of the Red. It was never as crowded. Taxis and street cars used the road more than pedestrians did. The real action, everyone knew, was on Desperation Avenue.

Severen did as ordered and the big screen suddenly filled with more fuzzy images, this time of a street filled with cabs of all kinds and littered with trash. International Street was, in Spider's opinion, one of the best places to do business in the Red. Tourists feared it because of its reputation, so it was nearly deserted most nights. Spider could see a few scattered residents loitering around their tiny shops or on street corners. He pointed to one of the images, where a man stood behind a large plywood structure with a sign atop it that read *Guns & Ammo*. Tables full of weapons surrounded the man on three sides. Even with the poor quality of the video, Spider could see the illegal phone implant blinking away on the man's left ear. "Who is that?"

Severen tapped a few keys and squinted at his screen. "I think it's Fast Dealer." He turned to Spider. "What—"

Spider cut him off. "Not now." He adjusted the headset's mike. "Tak? Fast Dealer's got a booth set up just past Inkwell. Get there." Spider pointed to the screen once more and turned to Thrash. "Get Fast Dealer on the phone right now."

Thrash tapped keys until she said, "Got him. On you, boss."

Spider began to speak into the mike. "Fast Dealer, this is Spider. Just listen. I've got a man headed your way with some heat behind him. What are you charging for a PK-31 right now?" He waited several seconds while the other man answered him. "I'll go a hundred more. But I need it now. My man is on the way to you." He snapped his fingers at Thrash while Fast Dealer replied. "And two full magazines to go with it." Another few seconds. "Done. Bill me." Spider looked up at the big screen and saw Fast Dealer flash him a thumbs-up and a grin.

"Tak? Fast Dealer's got a PK-31 and two full mags for you at his booth. When you get there—" He took a moment to stare at the screen, looking at the map. "—take the gun and move up International to Chadworth. Take it across Desperation to Hyde Street."

"Triad turf?"

"Just do it."

Takashi didn't answer, but Spider could see him moving on the map, out of the alley and onto International Street. He turned away from the screen and looked at Thrash. "Get me God."

"God's off-line right now," answered Thrash. "I already checked."

"Then get her online! This situation has gone to fuck way too quickly! Something is going on and I want to know what it is right fucking now! Get her!"

The two tech-monkeys began typing furiously. Spider ignored them while he stared at the screen. Thrash was still following Takashi using the Red's street cameras, terrible as they were. Around him, the loiterers and the info-junkies and the hustlers began to clear out, sensing the heat.

~~~

Takashi kept one hand on Kimber as he led her down International. Fast Dealer's booth was in sight ahead of him. He figured the scene in the club had bought him a few extra seconds. Takashi holstered the pulse-pistol as the booth got closer.

Fast Dealer

Fast Dealer smiled his gap-toothed smile. "Nice night for a shootout, eh?" The accent was Australian.

"Gun," said Takashi. He had stopped in front of the booth now, with Kimber on his left.

Fast Dealer slid a greasy PK-31 across the booth's plywood counter, then added two magazines. "Full to the brim," Fast Dealer said, still smiling. "Good luck, mate."

Takashi racked the PK-31's bolt, chambering a round. He stuffed the two extra mags into his pockets and turned to Kimber. "Run," he said.

She didn't need to be told a second time. Given the freedom, she took off down International. Most of the people had cleared out now, giving them more room to move around. As long as she stayed in his sight, he figured it was okay.

He chanced a look behind him, and saw the mib coming around the corner. A burst from the machine gun in his hands drove the man back around the corner and kept him there. Takashi caught up to Kimber and took her hand, gentler this time. She picked up the pace, and so did he.

~~~

Agent Ellis approached the corner with his weapon drawn and ready. He knew the Jap and the girl weren't far ahead of him. He knew where he was in the city as well. This was Triad territory. Here, he knew, the Chinese gang ruled the streets, keeping watch over their domain. He had to be careful.

He peaked around the corner and nearly received a face full of bullets for his trouble. The weapon sounded like a machine gun, much higher caliber than his pistol. Somehow the Jap had gotten help. Ellis was unsure if the machine gun would tip the balance in the Jap's favor. He already knew the terrain better than Ellis did. Would the weapon make the difference?

Ellis waited a few seconds, then peered around the corner once more. This time, he was met by no gunfire, so he moved out from the corner and into the street. He could see a large booth filled with guns and staffed by a lone man with grubby hands and dirt on his face. Ellis took note of the weapons hanging on the booth and the racks of guns on either side of the grubby man. That must've been where the Jap got his new toy.

Ellis carefully moved down the street, approaching the weapons booth on his right. The grubby man behind the booth's counter flashed him a smile full of missing teeth and said, "Looks like you could use a better weapon than that SH15. Interest you in something?"

He considered it for only a moment. Why not level the playing field? Graves had been in possession of the only heavy weapon the small team had been tasked with for the operation. Ellis cursed himself for leaving such a sweet gun behind in Dragon's Tears, but he had had other problems to deal with at the time. Now, though …

Ellis eyed the weapons hanging or leaning around the booth. His eyes landed on a near-perfect copy of Graves' FM-240. He pointed to it. "That one."

The gun dealer behind the booth took the weapon down and slid it across the booth's dirty counter. Ellis could feel the fresh oil on the weapon's barrel as he picked it up. "Ammo," he said, and the gun dealer lifted two clips from below the makeshift counter, sliding them along beside the gun.

"Here you go," the gun dealer said. "All told, you're looking at eight hundred."

Ellis shot the gun dealer between the eyes with his SH15 and lifted the spare magazines, tucking them into his suit jacket. The gun dealer's brains were already cooling on the back wall of the booth, dripping down to form a puddle in the street. Ellis lifted the FM-240 and made his way down the street.

~~~

Chadworth wasn't far now. Takashi turned and fired another burst from the PK-31. He pulled Kimber with him around the corner onto Chadworth and scrambled behind the buildings. "Faster," he said, and she left him behind in seconds. He took longer, wanting to keep the mib back as long as he could. Maybe he'd get lucky and take the bastard out.

He reached the top of the street, where it connected with Desperation. Here, the crowds were thicker and the sound of gunfire was muted somewhat by the thump of music and the chatter of a thousand voices all speaking at once. Takashi dropped to one knee and raised the assault rifle to his shoulder, taking aim at the building's corner down the street. He waited for the mib to pop his head around the corner, then held the trigger down for two seconds. That should keep him back. Takashi leapt up and grabbed Kimber's wrist, then pushed through the crowds onto Desperation Avenue.

~~~

"I found God," Severen announced.

Spider pointed to a smaller screen on his right, still the size of a television. "Bring her up on this one."

Severen did as ordered. A second later, the image of God filled the smaller screen. Spider didn't wait for her to smile or say hello. Instead, he pointed an accusing finger at her. "What the hell did you get us into?" he shouted. "I've got mibs after my guy and your little refugee!"

A moment later, God asked, "MIBs? Real ones?"

"Looks that way. They're packing phony FBI badges and IDs. Their pictures don't spark anything from anywhere. Only explanation, right?"

"Where's your man?"

"Moving across Desperation on Chadworth, headed to Hyde Street." He backed up several paces and stared at the larger screen above his head. "What the hell are they after?"

"What do you think, Spider?" God retorted. "They want the implant!"

"What?" Spider was shocked. The implant? "But why? It's dead, it died as soon as—"

"Doesn't matter," God interrupted. "They still want it, and probably the girl too. The same reason everybody else wants them. You know what it is, Spider. The body's neural energy powers the implant, that's why it goes radio-dead when you pull it out. It's like a tracking chip, but far more powerful. That kind of technology could revolutionize computing power. It's nanotech on a scale we can't even begin—"

"Yeah, yeah, whatever. Did you know she was being followed or tracked or whatever?"

"After what happened to Trace, there was a high probability that—"

Spider shot her the finger. "Fuck you, God." He turned to Thrash. "Cut her."

The screen went dark.

He turned away and focused on the big screen. Takashi was still making his way down Chadworth, crossing over Desperation Avenue. Hyde Street wasn't far away.

"Come on," he whispered to himself. "Come on."

~~~

Ellis had lost sight of his targets, but as he crept down International, he knew there was only one way for them to go. He swept Chadworth with the rifle before he continued down it. Still no sign of the two. Until he reached Desperation Avenue.

He could see the two, just now making their way across the street. Around them, crowds of people moved up and down the street, going about their own business. No one seemed to mind that he was carrying an automatic weapon in his hands as he passed a group of Jahdanka Girls loitering nearby. He ducked behind a black Halperin Hyperion in the street and crept around it as he found his targets once more.

They were now across the street and moving down Chadworth, passing eateries and shops along the way.

Ellis stood up and jogged across the street, keeping the weapon low so as not to cause a scene. Even one scream could cost him this opportunity. So he hid the weapon as best he could and kept moving until he, too, was across the street.

The Jap and the girl were about three-quarters of the way down the block, almost to Hyde Street. Ellis couldn't allow them to get any farther.

Ellis raised the weapon to his shoulder and sighted down the barrel. Too much movement for a kill shot, but if he could get the Jap down and panic the girl into running, he'd have no problems. A quick shot to the Jap's head, and he'd find the girl with ease. She had no training, no knowledge of the area around her. It would be almost too easy.

Ellis switched the weapon down to semi-auto, then drew a bead on the Jap's back and pulled the trigger.

~~~

Takashi managed to make it through the crowds to the other side of the street. Kimber was beside him all the way. Chadworth led them past several shops and small eateries, the smell of sushi and dumplings and noodles filling the air. Takashi dodged past several circuiters waiting for a seat outside one of the noodle houses, pulling Kimber with him into the street. Behind them, he could see no sign of the mib.

"Boss," Tak said, "I've lost the mib. No visual."

"Keep moving," came the reply.

Takashi stepped onto the sidewalk, using the circuiters as cover if the mib showed his face. They were almost there.

Takashi felt the bullet slam into his back before he heard it. The Kevlar he wore beneath his suit stopped it from penetrating, but it hurt like hell. Takashi pushed Kimber to his left against one of the buildings and swung around, bringing the PK-31 up to bear.

Down the street, the mib had fired into the circuiters to get them out of his way; Takashi could see a body on the ground, and a sobbing figure kneeling over it. One of the circuiters made a grab for the mib, but the man was shoved against the eatery's front window and shot twice in the head.

Takashi waited for the mib to move off the sidewalk around the circuiters, then he opened fire, emptying the mag. He didn't wait. He ejected the spent clip and shoved a fresh one in, slamming it home. He racked the bolt, then leaned down and grabbed Kimber by the left wrist. He didn't need to say anything. She knew. Without a word, she got to her feet and followed him down the block to Hyde Street.

Once there, Takashi pointed to his left. There was a basement stairwell there, filled with shadows. Takashi moved Kimber across the street to the stairway, ducking into it. He leveled the machine gun at the intersection, now on his left, and waited. He didn't think it would take long.

He was right.

As the mib proceeded cautiously around the corner, Takashi let loose a short burst. The mib backed up onto Chadworth and used the building as cover. *Shit*, Takashi thought. He had meant for the mib to be dead with that blast. He was not interested in a drawn-out shooting match at this point.

~~~

Ellis had blown it. The best opportunity he had to take out the Jap bodyguard, and he had fucked it up. All because of the crowd. And then that idiot punk had tried to take the gun from him. This whole thing was turning right back around on him, forcing him into a corner. He had orders. If he didn't complete the mission, there was no telling what would happen. In a job like his, you didn't get a pink slip. You got a bullet. And that was not what he wanted right now.

Ellis moved down Chadworth, mumbling curses to himself. No one else got in his way.

As he reached the intersection with Hyde Street, his instincts kicked in and he slowed his pace. The gun dealer had sold the bodyguard a modern equivalent of the AK-47. The weapon did not jam, it did not malfunction, and you could shit in the mechanism and it would still fire. One burst would shred him. He backed himself up against a massage parlor on the corner and checked his own weapon, switching it to full-auto. He leaned out with the weapon and—

A burst of fire drove him back.

He couldn't tell where the shots were coming from, but he had seen several large stairwells that probably led to basement apartments and the like. More than likely, the Jap bodyguard and the girl were hiding in one of them.

Ellis took a breath and leaned out from behind the building, the FM-240 already raised, and fired a burst.

~~~

The mib fired from behind the building, his rounds striking the concrete stairs as Takashi ducked behind them. He had to think. He had to figure this out. "Any ideas, boss? I can't exactly wait for the Triads to notice us."

"Get out of there before you get pinned down."

"Might be too late." Takashi ducked out and fired another burst at the corner. The mib was already there, and he fired as well. Takashi felt the rounds zip past his face. He fired again. The mib dove out from his cover and sprinted across the street, ducking behind his own stairway.

Takashi turned and glanced at Kimber. "Do not move," he said slowly. "Stay right here."

She nodded silently. Then he did something he had never done before. He slipped the pulse-pistol from its holster and handed it to the girl. "Ready to go. Just point and pull the trigger. Three-round burst. Hold it tight." Another nod.

Takashi took a breath, then leaned out from his cover and fired at the stairwell, only twenty yards away. Then

CARTER JOHNSON

he stood up and sprinted forward, firing a burst here and there. The mib ducked out, and one of the bursts caught him in the shoulder. He dropped to the sidewalk with a grunt. Takashi didn't wait. There would be no eloquent speeches or interrogations, no matter what he wanted. This man needed to be killed in order for him to complete his own mission. Takashi raised the rifle and finished the job, stitching bullets across the mib's chest.

As he turned away from the dead MIB, there was a burst of gunfire from behind him. He ducked away, throwing himself into the stairwell where the dead mib had hidden only seconds before. He checked the magazine in his PK-31. Half-full. He slammed it home and peaked out, taking in the scene before him in seconds.

Down the block, he could see four men carrying assault rifles. Each wore a dark suit, and each was the size of a house. They raised their rifles and took aim once more.

Takashi dove out of the stairwell and ran as fast as he could, covering the twenty yards in seconds as these new adversaries advanced up the street. He ducked down and grabbed Kimber's hand, then fired a long burst at the oncoming men, nearly emptying the clip. The men scattered to stairwells and doorways, just as he hoped.

Takashi didn't say a word as he pulled Kimber from the stairway and ran down the street with her hand in his. He aimed the rifle behind him and fired randomly, just trying to keep them back. In between the bursts, he could hear his boss on the line, yelling for a sit-rep.

"I'm busy, boss," he managed, "give me a few."

The reply was drowned out by gunfire from behind them. Takashi tried to run faster, but he was already giving it everything he had.

~~~

Spider turned to Thrash. "Who the hell is shooting at him now?"

"Not the Triads." Thrash pulled up a particular camera view on the big screen. "See? Triads don't dress like that, and they are nowhere near that size on average. Those are big boys right there."

No shit, Spider thought. So what was the deal? "Get God back on the line." The fact that he had said "fuck you" to her and cut her off was just more water under the bridge; she'd have done the same thing to him if the situation was reversed. "Make it snappy."

"She's calling you right now, boss." Thrash punched several keys, then the image of God was once again on the smaller screen to Spider's right. She did not look happy.

"You've got trouble, Spider," God said, her face full of gloom.

"I'm looking at it right now. Who the hell are these guys?"

"Russians. Wetwork specialists."

"Wait, are you saying those are Russian government agents?"

"Probably ex-Spetsnaz guys that followed the Iron Giant into office. He loves those types of guys. They'll kill your man and take what they want."

"No shit. I thought you were smart. Are they after the implant, too?"

God nodded. "And the girl, more than likely. Abductees are disappearing more and more."

"How did they find him?"

"I'm working on that—"

"Work faster. My guy is out there alone with no back-up."

"I'll do what I can." She ended the transmission, and Spider turned away from the monitor screen. He looked up at the larger screen above him, taking in the cameras and the map. Takashi was moving up Hyde Street now, but it was strange. By now, with all the gunfire, he should have Triads streaming out of every door, looking to put two in his head as well as the Russians. So where the hell were they?

"How's it going, Tak?" he said into the headset mike. "Tell me something."

"Moving," Takashi replied. "Where the hell is the Triad response, boss?"

"Don't know. Keep going. Maybe they're out to lunch right now."

"Not funny."

Spider focused on the screen. "Try to thin the ranks if you can, Tak."

"Copy."

Spider shook his head, silently cursing to himself. This operation was going to hell far too quickly for his liking.

8

TAKASHI DIDN'T UNDERSTAND. Why wasn't the plan working? It was a perfectly reasonable idea. But where were the Triads? This was their neighborhood. The gunfire should've drawn them all out, ready for war. He should be running from a gun battle between these Russians and the Triad soldiers. Instead, the apartment blocks and businesses around him were silent. He could see people in a few of the windows around him, but that was all.

He shook his head as he ran, grunting. If the Triads weren't going to come out and play, then he had to make a move himself. "I'm heading for Desperation, boss. Need some high ground."

"What do you have in mind, Tak?" Spider asked, his voice distant in the ear piece.

"I'm improvising." He took Kimber by the hand and ran her across the street, ducking behind a staircase as the Russians opened fire once more. The road was curving now, following the same path as Desperation on his right. He fired another burst behind him and took off, still holding Kimber by the hand. The next intersection, Hyde and Grandhower, wasn't far now.

Grandhower was filled with more shops and small restaurants. Takashi ducked into a noodle house with Kimber at his side. He pushed past an old woman behind a counter and made his way into the kitchen, despite the old woman's shouts. He used the rifle to smack a waiter in the face when the man got in his way, but other than that, he made it through with no problems.

The back of the restaurant led to an alley filled with more trash. He climbed over it, with Kimber at his side, and made his way to a rusting fire escape. He indicated it with the rifle. "Up you go."

"Will it hold us?"

"One way to find out. Go."

Kimber began to climb the ladder. "Faster," Takashi urged, and the girl sped up as much as she could, the pulse-pistol clutched in one hand. Takashi began the climb behind her, keeping one eye on the noodle house's back door. The Russians would figure out where he had gone with ease. Pinning them down in the restaurant might buy him some time. "Keep going," he said. "All the way."

Kimber reached the first landing and began to run up the stairs to the next one. Takashi followed her, then took up a position on the third-floor landing. "I'll meet you at the top," he said. Kimber stared at him with fear in her eyes for only a moment before she continued up the stairs, disappearing on the ninth landing.

Takashi raised the PK-31 and flicked the selector switch down to semi-auto. He needed to make every round count now.

Thirty five seconds later, the noodle house's back door flew open, but no one emerged. Takashi sighted down the rifle's barrel and waited. A few seconds later, one of the Russians stepped out into the alley, his weapon raised. Takashi could now see that he was carrying a Chinese GFT-95, modified with a shorter barrel and tricked out with laser sights and a scope. Takashi waited another few seconds until a second Russian stepped out the door, carrying an identical rifle. The two men stayed close to one another, each covering one side of the alley. Takashi picked the second Russian and fired two rounds at the man's head.

He did not wait to see the impact.

Takashi turned slightly and fired three rounds at the first Russian's chest, dropping the man in a flash.

Both Russians were down now. Takashi trained his rifle on the doorway and put two rounds through the opening. Then he leapt to his feet and scrambled up the fire escape, turning his head slightly to look below him. There was no movement. When he reached the top, he peaked over the edge to see the third and fourth Russians exiting the noodle house with their guns raised. He smiled to himself and left the sight behind him.

Kimber was a few yards away, staring over the side of the building at Desperation Avenue below her. She faced him and asked, "What now?"

Takashi indicated the next building. "They'll be coming. Get to the next building and keep going." He checked the PK-31's remaining magazine. Only ten rounds left. The weapon would be useless soon enough. He jammed the magazine back into the receiver. "Come on." As he moved, he tapped his ear piece. "You still with me, boss?"

"Still here," came the reply.

"I got two. I'm on the roof of some apartment building on Grandhower, moving towards the next building."

"Good. See if you can get those other two."

"Copy that."

~~~

"God's on the line for you, boss," said Thrash. "Putting it up now."

Spider turned his head to the right and God appeared on the small screen. "Tell your man to ditch his GPS unit. He's been hacked."

"Shit," Spider said, then he spoke into the headset. "Tak, ditch your GPS now. That's how they're tracking you."

"Roger," came the terse reply.

Spider turned back to the screen. "You want to tell me what's going on?"

"The Nowhere Kids," God answered.

"Fuck," was all Spider could manage. He had questions, but he couldn't voice them because his brain was running too fast for his mouth to catch up. He knew who the Nowhere Kids were, everybody did. They were a black-hat hacker collective that operated in total secrecy and worked for anyone who would hire them, including known terrorist organizations. Nobody knew who or where they were, only that the group had pulled off some of the most successful and crippling hacks of the last decade. The Nowhere Kids had, on several occasions, put down their computers and picked up arms. Just last year, they had inadvertently started and participated in a riot in what remained of Los Angeles, protesting the Draconian policies of the California Unified Police Department. The protest had led to a gun fight which killed seventeen police officers and nearly forty members of the group.

God continued. "They hacked the unit and they sold the location to the Russians and who knows who else. For all we know, every group in the world is after your man right now."

Spider frowned. "They don't care about him. They just want the implant. And the girl."

God nodded. "That's correct. I'll do what I can from here to get your back, Spider."

"I appreciate that. All I want is to get my man back here with the girl and be done with this."

Instead of hanging up, God stayed on the line this time. Spider could hear the tapping of keys coming from her end, and he wondered just what it was she was up to. God stopped her tapping after several seconds and looked up at him. "I've traced the hack back to a server that's run by Jeremiah Nightshade." Spider knew the name. According to rumor, it was the moniker of the self-styled leader of the Nowhere Kids. Spider had never met the man personally, but he knew that God harbored a strong dislike for him. "In exactly forty-three seconds, it'll be offline. Permanently." Then God let loose a string of Japanese swear words so long that Spider couldn't keep up. "What is it?" he asked, when she had finished ranting.

"He's tracking them. Or they are. Whatever. They've got a keyhole looking straight down at your man and the girl. They must be streaming his location to the Russians. They're on this in real time. As soon as your man ditched his GPS, they pulled up the satellite view."

"How the hell do you know that?" Spider was sometimes taken aback by her abilities.

"You don't need to know how." Another smile, but this one grew into a grin. "That son of a bitch shot me in the stomach over ... something else you don't need to know about. I'm going to blow his nuts off." The smile disappeared and became a hard glare. "You and yours cover your man. I'm gonna put a stop to this shit right now." Then the transmission ended.

"Get her back!" Spider shouted, but Severen was already shaking his head.

"She's dark, boss. She's gone deep."

"Shit," Spider muttered, then shook his head. "Okay, fuck it. I guess we're on our own."

~~~

Takashi made his way across the rooftop. He was almost to the edge when he heard the sound of a shotgun being pumped in the shadows to his right. "That's far enough," someone said in Chinese.

Takashi stopped, dropping Kimber's hand. "Don't do anything," he whispered. "Let me handle it."

Kimber inclined her head slightly to indicate understanding.

A Triad soldier stepped out of the shadows, holding the shotgun in his hands. He smiled at Takashi. "The Russians want you bad." More Chinese. "Looks like I'm gonna get an extra payday."

"They paid you already?" Takashi asked, using English.

"Sure," the soldier answered, still using Chinese. "Why else would we let them wander through our territory firing off guns?"

So that settled it. The Triads had been paid off to stay away and let the Russians have him and the girl.

The Triad soldier moved closer to Takashi, using one hand to remove the PK-31 from Takashi's own. "They'll be here soon," the soldier said. "Say a prayer." Takashi waited until the soldier took a step to the right, then he lashed out with one fist, smashing it into the soldier's orbital socket, fracturing the bone. The soldier cried out, and his finger jerked on the shotgun's trigger, sending a blast across the building's roof. Takashi took the shotgun away easily enough, then let the soldier have a blast to the face.

He pumped the slide and lifted his PK-31 from the roof. Kimber had not moved the entire time. "Let's go," he said.

Before she could take a step, gunfire and shouts in Russian came from behind them. Takashi fired the shotgun until it was empty, forcing the Russians to split apart. He dropped the empty weapon and grabbed Kimber. There was no point in trying to make it to the next building. The Russians were too close. They would have to go down here, using the building's roof access.

The door was several yards to his left, buried in shadow. He broke it down with two forceful kicks, then dragged Kimber through the opening as more gunfire filled the air behind them. The stairwell was not properly lit, the bulbs dangling on bare wires from holes in the ceiling. But it was passable. There were no large obstructions that he could see. Kimber stayed on his right, holding the pulse-pistol in one hand.

Down and down they went. On the seventh floor, they could hear the two Russians shouting to each other two stories above them. This urged them both on, Kimber once again getting ahead of him. He let it go this time, until there was a burst of automatic fire from above that demolished the stairwell's cheap wooden railing. Kimber dove to the side as Takashi moved to the next landing.

On the fourth floor landing, the Russians let loose with another burst, but before Takashi could return fire, someone else did from the fifth floor. The Russians were momentarily engaged in a gun battle that would hopefully occupy them for a few minutes. Takashi pushed Kimber ahead of him as they hit the third floor landing.

By the time they made it to the first floor, Takashi could barely hear the two Russians. He guessed they were still on the fifth or sixth floor. A better head start than they had had before. Takashi shouldered past two info-junkies loitering around the building's front door, buried in their tablets.

Out on the street, Desperation Avenue was just as busy as before. "Back on the street, boss," Takashi said, and waited for a reply.

"Wait one."

"Don't have one to wait, boss. Where am I going? Back to the club?"

"No, lose the Russians first. Or kill them. We're working on that."

"Work faster." Takashi grabbed Kimber's wrist and bolted into the street, not caring about the squealing tires or the shouts he received.

"Can you make it back to Hyde Street? I might have an idea."

"I think so, boss."

"Good. Take it all the way to Lexington. Run them straight into Haitian territory."

"Think it'll work this time?"

"The Haitians don't make deals with Russians, government or otherwise."

On the other side of Desperation Avenue, Takashi found himself in the midst of several cyberpunks who were arguing over something or other. He pushed past them with Kimber at his side. When one started to say something, Kimber flashed him the pulse-pistol before

Takashi could react. He smiled to himself and continued down the street.

The next intersection was Nakamora Drive. Takashi led Kimber onto the sidewalk and around a cluster of Harajuku Girls, gathered in front of an electronics store to watch a news broadcast. On Nakamora, he moved past a sushi bar and a poorly-maintained tap house that served nothing but imported beers from around the world. Takashi dismissed the tap house and moved on.

As they hit Hyde Street, Takashi took a moment for a quick look around. But the street was nearly deserted, save for a few cabs looking for work and two drunks who leaned against the stairwell of a building down the block. He pointed down Hyde Street and flashed a look to Kimber. "Same rules apply. Keep moving in that direction. If something happens to me, don't stop."

Another nod. She didn't waste her words, he had to give her that. Kimber held the pulse-pistol like she knew how to use it and followed him as he left Nakamora behind and crossed onto Hyde Street, the PK-31 held high and ready to fire. He still had two full clips left for the pulse-pistol, so at least he wasn't walking into Triad territory completely naked. Not that it would do much good. The Triads usually packed full auto. But every little bit helped.

Across the street, he got a better look at the layout ahead of him. Hyde Street was as deserted here as it had been a few blocks back. Nothing moved. Usually, there would be a thump of music or the chatter of drunken conversation as tourists stumbled off the beaten path or the Triads were in a celebratory mood. But tonight, the street was empty. The quiet that filled the air was unsettling in a place usually filled with activity.

Takashi followed Kimber down the street, letting her take the lead. The trouble would be coming from behind them, not in front. He kept the PK-31 ready, knowing the weapon would be empty and useless soon. He held onto it anyway.

"Russians are heading across Desperation." Spider's voice in his ear.

Takashi gripped the PK-31 tighter. "Copy."

"They're moving slow now. Looks like you spooked them." There was a moment of hesitation from Spider. "Scratch that," he said. "One of them is wounded. Looks like a shot in the leg. Not fatal, but slowing them down."

Takashi managed a smile. That gunfight in the stairwell had helped him more than he thought it would. Now the trick would be to simply stay ahead of them. Hyde Street, unlike Desperation Avenue, was poorly lit and filled with inky darkness on either side. Desperation Avenue received the attention it did because that was where the money was made. Nobody gave a shit about Hyde Street.

Takashi took Kimber's hand and raced her across the street, trying to stay in the shadows. "How am I doing, boss?"

"Russians are two hundred yards behind you now. Stay on course."

Takashi led Kimber around a cluster of metal trash cans, overflowing with rotting garbage. City trucks made it through here once a month, if they made it at all. Takashi felt the offal beneath his feet as he tried unsuccessfully to avoid it. Kimber slipped in it, but caught herself before she went down. Takashi helped her up, and the two continued to run.

The burst of gunfire behind them brought him behind a concrete stairway. The rounds ricocheted off the concrete behind him, kicking up dust and street crud and chips of concrete. Takashi stuck his head out just a few inches—

A gun blast brought his head back down as the stairs were riddled with bullets. But he'd seen enough. The two Russians were moving up the street on either side, covering left to right. If he could distract them long enough, he could take them both out. But it meant using the girl.

Takashi turned to her. "You're not going to like this."

Kimber said nothing, so he continued.

"See that car over there?" Takashi pointed down the block to the rusted-out shell of a ten-year-old Oberron. "I need you to run to it and hide behind it. Understand?"

She nodded. "Bait?" she asked.

"Bait," agreed Takashi. "Can you do it?"

"I'm gonna die if I don't, right?"

Takashi said nothing. The girl had a pretty good grasp on the situation.

Kimber nodded. "Tell me when."

Takashi leaned out of the stairway and took a good look.

The first Russian was moving up the street towards him, dragging his left leg slightly, while the second Russian was across Hyde Street. He seemed to be peaking into the alcoves and doorways set along the street as he moved past them. The two were only fifty yards behind them now. They were moving faster than before, even with the injury.

Takashi ducked back and pointed. "Straight to the car. They'll zero in on you and move that way. When they do, I'll take them out."

Kimber nodded.

"Go."

The girl leapt to her feet and sprinted into the street, pumping her arms as she moved. There was a shout of Russian, then gunfire followed her as she ducked behind the rusty Oberron's shell. Takashi counted to ten.

On three, Kimber ducked out and fired a burst from the pulse-pistol. Takashi was impressed.

On seven, one of the Russians returned fire, shattering the Oberron's remaining front window.

On nine, he began to stand up. On ten, he took aim at the nearest Russian, the one across the street, and fired three rounds.

The Russian's chest exploded, sending blood and matter flying in all directions. The Russian slumped to his knees, then fell over to his right. Takashi stepped out from behind the stairway and took aim. But even wounded, the other Russian was faster.

Takashi took a barrage of rounds to the chest, shredding his shirt and destroying his suit jacket. He felt the sting of each round as it bounced off his Kevlar, but the impact knocked him off-balance and he fell to the ground. The PK-31 slipped from his grasp and clattered to the concrete.

The Russian said something as he raised his assault rifle, words that were unintelligible to Takashi. He prepared himself to meet his ancestors, but the shot did not come.

Instead, he heard a burst from the pulse-pistol, and the Russian toppled backwards as his face disappeared in a spray of blood. Takashi could feel droplets landing on his face and neck, but he dismissed it. He'd had someone else's blood on him before. This was nothing new for him. He wiped splatters from his face and flung them to the street.

Kimber stepped out from behind the Oberron, still holding the pulse-pistol. When she saw the body, she vomited onto the street. Wiping her mouth, she joined him as he knelt before the first Russian's body.

Takashi tossed the PK-31 aside and lifted the GFT-95 from the dead Russian's hand. He checked the magazine and found it half-full. He felt along the Russian's coat, locating a spare magazine. This was tucked into the remains of his suit jacket. As he stood, he turned his gaze to Kimber. "You alright?"

She nodded. "I've never killed anyone before."

"Now you have." He made his way to the second Russian's body, ignoring the gore that met him as he knelt down. He pulled the clip from this Russian's machine gun and tucked it into his jacket. The man had nothing else to give him. Instead, he withdrew his smartphone and made his way back to the first body, snapping several pictures of the dead man's face. When his phone was back in its pocket, he said, "Russians are down, boss. Both of them."

"Tell me about it later. Get your ass back here."

"Copy that." He scanned the street. Still empty. But he was getting that feeling again. "Come on." Kimber stayed with him as he moved past the Oberron, the machine gun leading the way.

A bullet ricocheted off the dead car's rusted body, zipping past Takashi's face. "Contact!" he shouted, shoving Kimber to the ground. A second bullet hit the car, and Takashi found the shooter easily enough. A sniper, fourth floor window of an apartment building forty feet away. Takashi leveled the rifle and waited for the third shot. When it came, he fired.

There was a scream of pain, then quiet. Takashi lifted Kimber to her feet and said, "Stay with me." He ran to the opposite side of the street, keeping the rifle trained on that particular window. "Got a sniper, boss," he whispered. "Left side of the street, fourth floor, twenty yards up."

"Keep moving," came Spider's reply. "Don't stop now. You're almost there."

Takashi did not respond. Instead, he kept his focus on the window. When the sniper did not return fire, he began to lower the weapon. A mistake.

Behind him, the front doors to apartment buildings on both sides of the road burst open, and Triad soldiers swept into the street. They carried guns, knives, baseball bats, anything they could find. The air was suddenly full of their noise. Despite their ragged attire, each wore an article of colored clothing designed to signify their allegiance to the Triad. Takashi had no trouble figuring out who they were.

"Triads are out, boss," he said. "Dead Russians mean open season."

"God damn it," Spider hissed. "Alright, now you're in the zone, Tak. Get to Lexington. I'll make the call."

"Roger." Takashi turned and fired a long blast behind him, scattering the Triads to either side of the street, but also drawing their fire. He had maybe fifty yards between himself and the girl and the Triad soldiers. He had to better that lead. Grabbing Kimber by the hand, he said, "Run."

She was used to it by now, and followed along beside him as he took off down the street. Bullets whizzed past them and struck the buildings around them. Takashi fired another burst behind them, not bothering to aim. He hoped this plan the boss had would work.

~~~

Spider felt the familiar sensation creeping up his fingertips towards his brain. The stress was getting to him. He needed a cigarette. There was no smoking allowed in the Hive as it could damage the equipment, and Spider knew he couldn't walk out the door until he was sure that Takashi was safe and headed back here.

That was a lie, his mind told him, a rationalization. He knew he was more concerned for Kimber than for Takashi. The Japanese man had lived in the Red for years now, and he knew how to take care of himself. Kimber was a traumatized abductee who had just been dropped into a situation over which she had zero control, and was now running for her life from Russian government agents and Triad soldiers. Not an unusual night for Takashi, but completely out of the ordinary for Kimber.

Spider ran a hand through his hair. "Anything?"

Severen shook his head. "Nada. God's gone deep, if she's even online at—"

"She's online," Spider said with conviction. "She's just hiding right now. Find her."

"On it, boss."

Spider turned his head to the big screen and checked the District cameras. Fuzzy images showed him Takashi and the girl moving up Hyde Street. They only had a few more blocks to go until the demarcation line. Without taking his eyes off the screen, he said, "Get me Jimmy J on the line. Now." He didn't care which tech monkey carried out the order. When he turned, both were staring at him. "I gave an order. Move it."

"Jimmy J, boss?" This from Severen. "You sure?"

"My people are walking into his territory with angry Triads behind them. Since the Triads killed his boss earlier tonight, I figure Jimmy J might want a little payback." He grinned.

Severen tapped keys for several seconds, then gave Spider a nod. "All yours," he said.

Spider slapped a smile on his face and crossed his arms. "Jimmy J, how are you doing tonight?"

The replying voice sounded like a bulldozer running over a fire engine, and was filled with malice. "What do you want, Spider? I'm busy."

"I know. I saw the news. Sorry about Papa Batuu. He was a good man."

"Save it, Spider. Tell me what you want."

"I've got a proposition for you."

"I'm not in the mood tonight. I've got bigger fish to fry."

Spider's smile became genuine. He was going to enjoy this. "I know. And that's why I'm coming to you with this. Takashi and a … refugee are on Hyde Street. They're being chased by an unknown number of Triads packing enough jazz to take on an army." An exaggeration, to be sure, but he needed the extra weight the words packed. He stopped there and let Jimmy J digest the words.

"And you want my help?"

"Actually, I just thought you might want a little payback tonight, that's all. Helping me out is just the cherry on top." He waited another second, then added, "I'd owe you one, Jimmy. A big one."

The other man was silent for several moments as he mulled the idea over. There was a noise on the line while Jimmy J cleared his throat. "Get your people across the demarcation line, and I'll take care of the rest."

"Done. Thanks, Jimmy. Like I said, I owe you."

"Yes you do. But I'm willing to let it slide tonight, just this once. I'm itching to splatter some Triad brains on my street." The call was ended.

Spider snapped his fingers at the tech monkeys. "Get Tak back."

Thrash tapped keys. "You're on, boss."

"Tak," Spider began, "I just got off the phone with Jimmy J. Get your own ass and the girl's over the line and he's got you. Bring the Triads straight to him."

"Got it, boss. Then what?"

"You know what."

"Copy." Takashi was silent once more.

Spider turned away from the screen. "Now we cross our fingers." He turned back before they could see the look in his eyes.

~~~

Takashi dumped the empty clip and shoved a new one into the assault rifle, racking the bolt. They had been running flat out for ten minutes, getting closer and closer to Lexington. It was only three blocks now. He fired another burst behind him, ducking behind a parked taxi with Kimber. He turned and fired at several Triad soldiers, not caring if he killed or wounded them. He just needed the time. Then he grabbed Kimber and kept moving.

As he crossed an intersection, not caring which street it was, his ears began to detect new sounds coming from in front of him. He tried to separate these new sounds from the noise behind him. It sounded like whoops of joy and the sound of large trucks moving. At least, he hoped that was what he was hearing.

If it was, the Haitians were mobilizing now.

Takashi chanced a quick look behind him. The Triads were now sixty or seventy yards behind him. They assumed, since they had control of the neighborhood, that they also had control of the situation. A true tactical error, to be sure. All he had to do was outrun them.

The street rose beneath him as he made his way up an incline, the apartment buildings and shops a blur as he moved. Kimber was still right beside him, her breath coming in ragged gasps now. She was losing steam. Truthfully, so was he. Adrenaline still pumped through his blood stream, but he could feel fatigue settling into his muscles. Just a little more, he told himself.

Ahead on his left, Takashi could see the door of an apartment building open up. He knew what was coming. "Shit," he said, and raised the GFT-95. As Triads began to pour from the building, he opened fire, spraying the building's front with bullets. Triads screamed and dropped to the concrete, some of them rolling down the stairs to the street below. Others dived away and hid as Takashi emptied the clip. He reloaded the weapon, but not fast enough. As he and Kimber passed the building, the soldiers returned fire. Takashi was lucky. Kimber was not.

A round caught her in the shoulder as she tried to move away, knocking her backwards. She cried out, but Takashi was there. He gave the wound a quick look and determined it was not fatal. She would need a doctor, but not immediately. They still had time.

Takashi helped her to her feet without a word, firing at the Triads who joined their brothers in arms as the group swept up Hyde Street. He shoved her ahead of him and fired again.

The road curved up and to the left, and they followed. Kimber's shoulder was bleeding freely now, he could see. She would need a tourniquet at the very least to slow the blood loss, but there was nothing else he could do for her. And even that, he could not do here. That would require stopping, and if they stopped, they'd be dead in ten seconds.

Takashi kept her in front of him, looking over his shoulder as the Triads tried to get him in their sights. They weren't stupid. They knew taking him out would put the girl at a disadvantage. She didn't know the area like he did, and she had no training.

They crossed a second intersection, and Takashi could see life continuing on Desperation Avenue. There was always money to be made. He wished he was there right now instead of here, taking fire. He could use a cold beer. Tsing-Tao, not the bullshit domestic beers. Chilled in a freezer for ten minutes. Served with a frosty mug, the way he liked it. But there would be time for that later. He was not dying in the middle of Hyde Street tonight. Not tonight.

Kimber grunted as her shoulder moved unexpectedly. He could see the pain in her eyes, but right now it didn't matter. She was tougher than she looked, he knew that now. If she could hold on just a little longer, they'd be out of the woods. "Pick up the pace," he whispered, and she did.

Now Lexington Street was in sight, and Takashi felt a grin spreading across his face as the demarcation line got closer.

Decade-old Desperado pick-up trucks were parked nose-to-nose on the street, three deep. Takashi could see Haitians with AK-47s standing in the beds of the trucks, as well as in front and behind them. His eye caught the snipers on the rooftops, armed with McClusky DM-8s fitted with scopes and silencers. Not that it would matter. They'd hear this gunfight in Cleveland, the way things were going. He picked out a large .50-caliber machine gun mounted in one of the truck beds. The man behind the weapon stepped back, then jumped from the truck bed and began to walk towards the street.

This was Jimmy J.

Takashi dragged Kimber toward the man, still wearing that grin. "Jimmy J. Good to see you."

The Haitian man returned the smile, his eyes sparkling. "I can see your relief, Takashi." He indicated the Triads closing behind him with a chin-jut. "That your party?"

"It was. Now it's yours."

Jimmy J's smile deepened. "Get out of here, Tak. We got this."

Takashi inclined his head. "With pleasure."

Jimmy J pointed to his left, Takashi's right, and said, "Take Lex out. You've got clearance."

"Thanks, Jimmy. See you around." Takashi handed the GFT-95 to the Haitian man. "Spoils of war." Then he took Kimber by the hand and began to run to his right, up Lexington Street.

~~~

The smile on Spider's face was so wide that it hurt. "Split it," he said. "Show me Tak and the girl, but keep one view on Lexington." He chuckled. "And get me some popcorn. This is going to be good."

Thrash laughed to herself behind him, which only deepened Spider's grin. The large screen split once more, displaying a grainy image of Takashi and Kimber moving up Lexington towards Desperation on the left, and a similar image of Lexington Street. Jimmy J had climbed back into the truck bed and was behind the big machine gun once more.

"Take 'em out, Jimmy," he whispered.

Without sound, he couldn't tell if the Triads fired first or not. The gang war between these two sides had escalated in the last few months, to the point that any Triads found across Lexington were returned to their own turf in pieces. Same deal if the Haitians were found in Triad territory. Maybe tonight would settle it, once and for all.

Jimmy J fired the .50-caliber, spraying Hyde Street with rounds. His soldiers opened fire as well. Spider pointed. "Show me the other side of Lex." The screen divided once more, now displaying a shot of Triad soldiers being cut to pieces. He could see that Jimmy J was taking losses as well, but the .50-caliber more than leveled the playing field. Jimmy J could've done it by himself if he wanted to.

Spider let the show run for a few more seconds, then shook his head. "Alright. That's enough. Follow Tak." He spoke into the headset. "Tak? How's it going?"

"Five by, boss. Girl's been hit, though."

"Is it bad?"

"Shoulder wound. She's bleeding heavily."

"Get her to Doc Medran's. Four blocks up Desperation on your left."

"Copy that."

"I'll make the call and get you to the head of the line. For Christ's sake, be careful, Tak. We don't have a full handle on all this yet."

"I hear you, boss. I'm on it."

"Call me when you get there. We've got you on the cameras, so we're still watching."

"Tak out." The call was ended.

Spider turned to Thrash and Severen. "Remind me to send Jimmy J a basket of muffins from that place at the corner of Preston and Child. Call off the red alert. Tell Quartez and the girls to stand down. We're in the clear for now."

Severen began to type and speak quietly into his own headset.

"Anybody find God yet?" Spider asked.

Thrash shook her head, the circuitry jingling in her ears. "Still zippo. I don't know if she's online, boss."

"Keep at it. Let me know something." He crossed his arms and turned back to the screen. "Somebody get Doc Medran on the line."

9

TAKASHI TUGGED AT his tie until it unknotted itself.

He and the girl were stopped on Lexington between Hyde and Desperation, just outside a cyberpunk clothing store. He wound the tie around her shoulder, cinching it tight then re-knotting it. "Too tight?"

Kimber shook her head. "It's good."

"Alright. Come on." He took the pulse-pistol from her hand and holstered it. It was bad form to flash your jazz on Desperation. It scared the tourists away, along with their money.

They moved away from the clothing shop, and Takashi could hear gunfire behind him. He smiled as the big .50-caliber opened up. He would've liked to stay for a few moments, not to watch the show but to cap off a few of the Triads himself. Assholes.

Kimber looked behind her at the sound of the shots. "Should we run?"

Takashi shook his head. "That part's over now. Forget them. The Haitians will take care of them for the time being. We need to get you to a doctor."

"Is that where we're going? A doctor?"

"Yes. When we hit the street, stay with me. Same as before. Hold onto my jacket if you have to."

They reached the intersection, and it was crawling with people. Takashi stepped onto the sidewalk, making sure Kimber was still with him. Blood dripped from the ends of her fingers, but it was less than before. The tourniquet was doing something, at least.

A shop down the street was blasting a J-Pop song, the same Yumi tune he had heard live only … what? Half an hour ago? It seemed like longer. It always did, he told himself. There were Jahdanka Girls gathered around the shop's entrance, dancing to the beat. Takashi weaved around them, keeping Kimber just behind him. If something was going to happen now, it would come from the front. Desperation was too packed now to attempt anything else. Besides, they all wanted the girl alive.

The J-Pop song faded away, and the sounds of the Red replaced it. Car horns, shouts, random gunfire, the rattle of rebuilt heating units working overtime in apartment windows. Takashi took to the street as he moved around a street vendor selling kabobs and noodles and sushi, then he was back on the sidewalk. Kimber took hold of his jacket.

Thankfully, he managed to get Kimber the four blocks to the Doc's without any more incidents. The streets were packed at this time of night, which wasn't unusual. He used the crowds to move down the street and remain anonymous, blending in wherever he could. The blocks passed quickly this way, and they arrived at Doc Medran's self-styled office in under ten minutes.

There were several people in line ahead of them when they pushed the plastiglass door open and stepped inside. The clinic was off the books, by appointment only, but that didn't stop people from coming in off the streets, people that lived here and knew about the place. Doc Medran tried turning them away, but they returned again and again. Some would wait in this lobby until they gave up. Others would find a way to get the money and come back.

Takashi pushed past several people on his way to the front of the line. A circuiter was behind the counter, dressed in her finery. Takashi slapped a smile on his face as he stepped up. "Urgent appointment with the Doc. A call was made a few minutes ago."

The woman looked him up and down, taking in his tattered suit. "For you?"

Takashi shook his head, then waved his hand behind him. Kimber was there in an instant. "For her." He pointed to Kimber's shoulder.

The circuiter made no indication that she cared either way. "Come on back. Room 2." She turned away from him. "Next."

Takashi held Kimber's hand as he led her through a doorway and into the clinic's rear. The walls were dirty, paint flecking off here and there. It had once been green, but was now mostly brown or black. Takashi located the room and led Kimber to it. Once they were inside, he called the boss.

"We're in," Takashi said. "Waiting on the Doc."

"Good." Spider's voice crackled with static. "Push him if you have to. He's already getting double as it is, so make sure he earns it."

"Got it, boss." Takashi hung up.

~~~

Spider breathed deeply through his nose and held it for three seconds, then expelled the air through his mouth. He did this twice more until he felt the tension in his muscles ease itself. "Jesus," he said, to no one in particular. He pulled the headset off and tossed it to Thrash, who caught it one-handed. "I need to grab a smoke after that. I'm stepping out. Anything happens, I'm right outside the door."

"Sure, boss," Severen said without looking up from his console.

Spider took the spiral staircase to the Hive's entrance, pulling the door open and stepping out into the night air.

He took the pack of American cigarettes from his pants pocket and shook one out. It was broken, so he tossed it over the side of the catwalk. The next one was bent slightly, but still in good shape. He jammed it into his mouth and sighed. Tonight had been more than he bargained for, that was for sure. He expected to be paid for all this trouble.

He took a Zippo from his pocket and flicked it to life. That first drag started the process, and he could feel the tension begin to leave his body. Spider leaned over the railing, staring out into the city.

Neon run-off from the street bathed the alley in half-light, giving it a soft red and green glow. *Looks like Christmas*, thought Spider, ashing his cigarette and taking another drag. He could see people crossing in front of the alley's mouth in groups of two or three or more. Jahdanka Girls, Future Goths, circuiters, cyberpunks, they were all there. The city, his city, was laid out below him like a smorgasbord. Anything you wanted could be found for a price, legal or illegal. Much of it was the latter. He tracked a young circuiter who walked past the alley alone.

Behind him, he could hear the club's back entrance open, and he turned around. Satoshi and Marisol were stepping out of the door, clutching Russian cigarettes in their hands. Marisol was talking, but he couldn't make

CARTER JOHNSON

out the words. Neither girl looked up at him as they settled in under the floodlight and lit up.

Sometimes it was nice to simply stand here and be invisible. Spider took another drag and watched the two girls as they talked. Marisol said something that made Satoshi cough up smoke and laugh. The two women began to speak animatedly to one another. Spider turned away and found his gaze landing on the alley's entrance once more. Now he could hear music thumping from the street, some dance tune that he was unfamiliar with. Then a group of hip-hoppers walked past the alley, one of them holding an ancient boom box radio that blasted out the tune. The hip-hoppers were gone in seconds, along with their music.

Spider took another drag and rolled the ash off the end of the cigarette.

Behind him, he heard the club's door open, then Satoshi and Marisol's voices disappeared. Spider smoked his cigarette while he stared at the Red, trying not to let thoughts of the girl invade his mind. He had been fighting them off for most of the night. Even in the shower, when he had allowed them space, he had still been trying to deny how he felt. But he couldn't, could he? Not anymore. Not after what had just happened.

Another drag, and the girl's face seemed to float past his eyes. Even in her sadness, her deep depression, she was still beautiful. There was a strength about her that she kept inside. All it took was one look into those eyes, and it was obvious. Her trauma had not killed her, unlike so many others with her affliction. She had continued on, refusing to let that be her life. She only looked meek on the outside.

The cigarette was soon finished. Spider flicked the butt into the alley and punched in his code, swinging the door open. Inside, he could hear music playing once more. Softer, though, with less of a dance beat. He found he kind of liked it as he wound his way down the stairs to the bottom level. "Talk to me," he said.

"Everything's good, boss," said Severen. "Same as when you left."

"Good. That's the way I like it." Spider slipped his headset back on and stood in front of the large screen, waiting for the call.

~~~

A few minutes later, the exam room door swung open and a man in his early sixties with white hair and a mustache walked into the room. Doc Medran hadn't been a licensed medical practitioner in nearly fifteen years, but his skills were put to good use in the Red almost every night. As long as you could pay. Takashi knew that his boss would take care of the details. That line about double meant exactly that.

Doc Medran

Doc Medran's voice was smooth and steady as he introduced himself to Kimber. Takashi, of course, he knew from previous visits. Kimber gave her name as 'Jennifer' once more, and the Doc accepted it without pause. "Jennifer," he began, "I'm going to need you to remove your shirt."

Kimber slipped the Thundercats t-shirt over her head and dropped it to the floor at her feet. The Doc instructed her to climb onto the exam table while he opened a nearby drawer and removed several items: swabs, a bottle of alcohol, a suture kit, and an extractor. He laid these items on a stainless steel tray which he set on the exam table beside Kimber.

Takashi waited patiently while Doc Medran cleaned the wound with swabs and alcohol, eliciting hisses and grunts from Kimber. Takashi gave her credit, though. She didn't cry out. And she didn't pull away at any point. She kept still while the Doc did his work.

Medran warned Kimber about the pain caused by the extractor while he held the device in one hand. Kimber told him to go ahead, and she winced when the machine began to do its work. The extractor dug the bullet out slowly but surely, while Kimber squeezed her eyes shut and bit her lower lip. But she kept silent.

After the wound was cleaned and the bullet removed, the Doc began to open the suture kit. Before he could get any farther, there was a knock on the door and a pink-haired nurse stuck her head onto the room. "Doctor Medran?" she asked timidly. "There's a call for you."

"I'm in the middle of something here, Dorian."

The pink-haired nurse named Dorian shook her head. "It's urgent, Doctor. Very urgent."

Medran harrumphed his way to his feet and shuffled out of the room behind the pink-haired nurse, pulling the door closed behind him.

Now Takashi was alone with Kimber.

He had been leaning against a wall in the corner of the room, but now he moved forward and stepped past Kimber, turning his eyes to her. "You okay?"

She nodded. "Fine. It hurts, but I'll be okay."

Takashi turned his eye to the door. "What the hell is taking him so long?"

Doc Medran returned two minutes later. Takashi was back in the corner, now with his hand on the pulse-pistol's grip. He relaxed slightly as the Doc gave him a small smile. Medran resumed his place in front of Kimber and began to sew up her wound.

Takashi kept his hand on the gun. In the three minutes since he had last spoken, all sorts of scenarios had begun to form in his mind. What if the Doc had sold them out? What if someone else had spotted them in the waiting area? Or that nurse who came in here? Every little paranoid thought bubbled to the surface, because it had been that kind of a night for him.

"I'm going to get some gauze to wrap that in," said Medran, and he stood up.

"Isn't there gauze in the cabinet there?" Takashi asked, and pointed across the small room to the same bank of cabinets and drawers from which Medran had pulled the suture kit.

The Doc smiled and said, "There should be, but my nurse hasn't been in here to restock the room. We've been busy."

Takashi crossed the room as Medran made his way to the door. He slipped out just as Takashi reached the bank of cabinets and drawers. Before he could open any of them, he heard the click of a lock on the other side of the door. "Son of a bitch," he muttered, then he whirled around and grabbed Kimber's hand. "Come on. Stay with me. This could get bad real quick." He drew the pulse-pistol and took aim at the door. When he fired, the lock burst apart and the door swung open into the room.

Takashi kicked it out of his way and led Kimber into the hallway. On his left, he could see Doc Medran and the pink-haired nurse talking to four men with bad haircuts and dark suits. They saw him, too. One of them shoved Doc Medran out of the way and drew a pulse-pistol of his own, taking aim at Takashi.

Takashi fired first, spraying the other end of the hallway with rounds as he pulled Kimber along with him. He saw the nurse and the Doc go down, along with the suit who had raised the gun to him, then he was gone down another hallway, this one leading to the front of the clinic.

Kimber didn't ask any questions as he pulled her along beside him, moving her along at his own pace. She kept up with him and did not impede his process. When he reached the lobby door, he kicked it open with one foot and shoved her through the doorway. He turned and fired two more bursts down the hallway as the suits rounded the corner behind him. Then he followed Kimber into the lobby and ran for the door.

Outside, Takashi touched the device still in his ear and waited as it dialed the Hive. When the line connected, he didn't wait for anyone to speak. "It's me. Got a problem. Medran sold us out to four suits with pulse-pistols. No idea who they are. Could be more mibs."

His boss answered him. "God damn it. Get her back here, Tak."

"You sure, boss?"

"Yes. Lead those fuckers straight into the alley behind the club. I'll take care of the rest." The line went dead.

Takashi took hold of Kimber's arm and dragged her into the middle of the street. Cars honked and lights flashed, but he didn't care. He just needed to disappear for a few minutes and make it back to the club. He hoped the boss had a good plan.

~~~

Spider slipped the headset off and tossed it to Thrash. "I've got my phone on me," he began as he moved towards the living quarters. "I'm going to pop an ear piece in, and you put me on a conference call with him and you when he calls back, got it? Call Quartez and tell her to meet me on the third floor. We may have a situation developing here that affects the girls." Then he disappeared.

Spider bypassed the cots and the shower and the small kitchen, moving instead to a steel door set into the concrete wall. He swung the door open and stepped into the Hive's armory. Here, he ran his eyes across weapons of every kind: pulse-pistols, assault rifles, submachine guns, even an honest-to-God rocket launcher. But what he wanted was on the wall straight ahead of him. The McClusky DM-8, fitted with a silencer and a night-vision scope. Spider took the weapon off the rack and began to load it.

Thrash appeared behind him. He could feel her eyes on his back. "What do you have in mind, boss?"

"This shit is getting out of hand. I'm tired of it."

"So what are you going to do?"

"Kill them." He hefted the DM-8 in one hand and a box of shells in the other, pushing past her out the door.

"You think this is the best move, boss? Tak can take care of—"

"I'm not worried about Tak." He passed the cots and kitchen and the shower on his way back into the main area. Severen was behind his own terminal, typing away. His eyes widened when he saw the rifle in his boss' hand.

"What's up, boss?" he asked.

Spider sidetracked to Thrash's console, where he picked up a small device and fitted it into his right ear. "Nothing to worry about." Spider began to climb the spiral staircase. "You two stay here." He swung the door open and held it with one foot as he walked out into the rain once more. He didn't care if it ruined this suit or not. He had other things on his mind.

Spider slid the box of shells into his pants pocket as he reached the other door. Here, he punched in his code and swung the door open, stepping into the club. He ignored the stage act, Dauphine and Vinyssa performing their cat-and-mouse routine in full costume, and continued through the second floor to the stairwell. He passed Satoshi on the stairs, who pointed to the rifle in his hand and asked, "What's up, Spider? Somebody piss you off?"

"Spread the word," Spider replied. "We have incoming. Get everybody ready."

Satoshi, never one to panic, simply nodded and said, "Consider it done." She continued down the stairs without another word.

Spider kept moving. As he had requested, Quartez met him on the third floor, wearing a quizzical look on her face. Until she saw the rifle. Then her eyes widened. "Tak's got heat on him," Spider said as he passed her. She moved quickly to keep up with him. "Get somebody on the back door to let him in when he gets here." He stopped for a moment, then turned to look at her. "This could get bad if we don't take care of it now, Diana. Real bad. Find a gun." Then he started walking once more.

Quartez didn't say another word. Instead, she turned and fled down the stairs, her silk kimono flapping behind her.

Spider crossed the large area, passing the bar. He stopped before an unmarked door with a simple deadbolt on it. He knew the door wasn't locked. Sometimes the roof was the most private place that a client could take his girl of choice, so Quartez left the door unlocked during business hours, which was to say all the time. Spider opened the door and stepped into a stairwell leading in one direction: up. He took the stairs two at a time until he reached the top, then threw the door open.

Red District air struck him in the face like a brick. Sometimes it made him want to gag. From up here, he could hear the sounds of Desperation Avenue, the shouting and the music and the car horns. He clutched the DM-8 as the door eased itself shut with a click behind him. He made his way across the roof, passing several marijuana plants cultivated by Quartez and the girls as well as a rooftop garden that was petering out for the season. It was a wonder anything could grow with this air, he thought to himself as he moved closer to the roof's edge. When he reached it, he checked the DM-8 once more to make sure it was loaded, even though he knew it was. Then he tapped the ear piece with a finger.

Thrash answered on the first ring. "I'm here, boss. Severen's got Tak on the District cameras."

"Good. Stay on the line for now."

"Copy that, boss."

Spider hunched down by the roof's ledge and raised the rifle, sighting it on the alleyway. If Tak had enough of a lead, he could get himself and Kimber into the club while whatever goon squad was chasing him was still on Desperation. They'd come down the alley and then Spider would finish this. He knew Thrash was right; Tak could handle himself. But he didn't have all the bullets in the world. Spider hadn't been lying before. He wasn't worried about Takashi. He was worried about Kimber.

Spider wiped rain from his face with one hand and waited.

~~~

Takashi kept a tight grip on Kimber's arm as he led her through the Red's heavy traffic. Even now, at this time of night, it was bad. But in that way, it was good. The cars and cabs were all either stopped or moving slow enough that he could dodge around them. He chanced a look over one shoulder and saw the suits coming out of the clinic's front door, weapons drawn.

Takashi pulled Kimber with him as he ran through the street to the sidewalk, trying to blend in with the crowds once more. Six blocks. That was all. He just had to make it six blocks. He could cut down the alley on Colton Street and get behind the club with ease. The problem was not letting the suits fall too far behind that they lost visual on him. He needed them to follow him.

His other problem, now that he thought about it, was location. He had no choice but to stay on Desperation. The Haitians were busy with the Triads on Hyde Street, and there was no telling what kind of Triad response he might run into on International Street. After the night he had had, the Triads would be itching to fill him with holes. No, he had to stay here and make his way through the crowds of people and the noise and the early-morning smog.

He heard shouting behind him and glanced over his shoulder. The goon squad was making its way down Desperation about thirty yards behind him. They had stumbled into a group of teen cycleheads and their hangers-on. Now, the goon squad was involved in what looked like the beginnings of a fist-fight. Takashi tried not to think about the cycleheads. He knew what the goon squad would do. As Kimber turned her own head to look, Takashi said, "Don't. You don't want to see this."

As he finished, he heard the first shots from behind him, followed by several screams. He didn't look back.

Kimber pointed to the intersection ahead of them. "Can't we duck onto that side street we were on earlier and get away from them?"

Takashi shook his head. "Triads are patrolling hard after the skirmish with the Haitians. We'd be killed. And we need them to follow us."

"What the hell for?" Kimber's voice had lost its meekness. Now, there was only a hard edge.

"The boss has a plan," was all Takashi would say. "Now come on. Keep moving."

Six blocks. Takashi looked over his shoulder and saw the goon squad moving closer. He grunted. He didn't want to do this, but he had no choice if he wanted to live. Takashi raised the pulse-pistol and fired two bursts behind him, aiming the weapon high so he wouldn't hit anyone. Right now, a gunfight wouldn't solve anything. He might take out one or two, but that would still leave two or three more depending on his shots. What he needed was panic, enough of it to slow the goon squad so he could make it back.

The crowds ducked and scattered every which way, exactly what Takashi had been hoping for. The downside was, the suits now had a clean shot at him. He took the opportunity to empty the pulse-pistol's clip behind him, not caring if he hit anything or not. As he turned back, he dumped the empty clip and reached for a fresh one, his last. He jammed it into the pulse-pistol and yanked the slide, chambering a round.

That was when Kimber did something that was completely unexpected: she tore the pulse-pistol from his hands and spun around, pointing the gun towards the suits. Before Takashi could stop her, she aimed roughly for the pursuing group and fired a burst, catching one of the suits in the chest. The man's jacket and shirt were suddenly full of bloody holes. He stopped in his tracks as if he didn't realize what was happening, reaching one hand up to touch a bullet hole. Then he dropped to his knees and his compatriots left him behind.

Kimber fired a second time, missing the remaining three suits but driving them behind a JR Cab idling in the street. Then Kimber tossed him the gun and started to run. "Thought you could use some help," she said.

"That's the second time you've done that tonight. Where did you learn to shoot like that?"

"I grew up in the post-mil South."

"That's not an answer."

"I know."

They crossed an intersection, pushing and shoving their way through the pedestrians. A Jahdanka Girl gave Kimber a shove, and Kimber demonstrated just how much she wasn't in the mood by slugging the Jahdanka Girl in the jaw and dropping her. Takashi took Kimber's hand and led her away from the scene as the Jahdanka Girl's friends came to her aid. Takashi raised one hand to his ear piece.

~~~

Spider could feel a slick coating of rain on his skin, the Red's air pollution mixing with the precipitation to create a thin paste-like substance that clung to his hands and the back of his neck. He could feel it growing across his body as more and more rain fell from the sky. He tried to ignore it, just as he tried to ignore the fact that a second suit was now ruined from one night's work.

He heard a light ringing in his ear and brought one hand up to touch the button on his ear piece. "What is it?"

"Tak's on the line," Thrash replied. "Sending him to you, boss." There was a brief hiss of static, then Tak's voice came on the line.

"Boss," Tak began, "we're coming down Desperation now. Five blocks out. Down to three out of four. Kimber took one out."

Spider kept the astonishment out of his voice. "Lead them right to me, Tak. I'm waiting."

"Copy that, boss."

Spider left the line open and readjusted his position on the roof. His knees were beginning to ache from the crouch he was in, but he ignored it for now. Knee pain would go away with a hot shower, his second of the night.

He heard some activity below him and glanced down.

Two circuiters were stumbling into the alley, a man and a woman. *Probably looking for a place to sneak a quickie,* Spider thought. This alley was as good as any, on a normal night. But tonight was not that. Spider whistled loudly to get their attention. The woman looked up, and the alley's meager light reflected across the black plastic tubes the woman called hair and the old wiring wrapped around her arms and shoulders. Spider shook his head slowly, making sure the woman could see the gesture. When she didn't stop moving, Spider swung the rifle around and took aim. Now the woman grabbed her companion's arm and began to pull him away. The man went reluctantly, his eyes still gazing at the alley's darkness as the woman dragged him back to Desperation Avenue.

Spider lifted the rifle and moved to his left a few inches, repositioning the weapon on the roof's ledge. He didn't bother to check his watch. Takashi could cover five blocks in a matter of minutes. Instead, he gazed through the rifle's scope and adjusted the focus. The rain wouldn't make things any easier, but his upbringing in post-mil Brooklyn had prepared him for events such as this. His aim was impeccable.

"How far?" he whispered, knowing Takashi could still hear him.

"Four and a half blocks. Coming up on Covenant on my left. See you soon, boss."

"How far back are the goons?"

"Twenty five yards. They have visual on me."

"Keep it that way."

Spider felt the familiar sensation creeping up his fingers to his arms. He wanted a cigarette. Spider cursed his own body for betraying him at a time like this. When he needed a smoke, his fingers and hands would tremble slightly, as if he was nervous. That alone could throw his aim off. Just because he had the high ground didn't mean this whole thing couldn't turn around and blow up in his face.

He brought his eye to the scope once more, preparing himself. He slipped one finger inside the trigger guard and felt the cold steel against his skin. He would get only one shot at this, one chance to pull it off. If he missed, the goon squad would have their own opportunity. Spider took several deep breaths to calm himself, forcing all thought from his mind. He needed to be clear for this.

Spider took one last breath, then closed his finger over the trigger. One or two ounces of pressure, and that would be it. Then repeat twice more. It sounded easy when he put it to himself that way. Maybe, with all the shit luck he had had tonight, it would be that easy. But he doubted it.

~~~

Takashi fired once more behind him as he and Kimber closed on the intersection, hoping to slow the goon squad once more. Kimber's shot with the pulse-pistol had gained them an advantage of one less man after them, but that was all. They still had three goons behind them. He tried to remind himself that he only had to make it another four blocks.

The shots came at the intersection.

Takashi felt two rounds strike his left leg just above his knee, tearing a hole in his femoral artery. He hit the ground on that knee, crying out in pain. Kimber was there, trying to lift him to his feet. "Come on," she said. "We're almost there."

Takashi shook his head and pointed below him. "Won't make it. I'll slow you down." Blood was pooling rapidly beneath his leg and body. It seemed to be running out of him as if it were trying to escape. Kimber knew he was right, but she refused to acknowledge it. Takashi reached into his torn jacket for the plastic tube and pressed it into her palm. "Take this and get back to the club. I'll keep them here." Then he removed his ear bud and passed it to her. "Boss is still on the line. Go." He gave her a shove and lifted the pulse-pistol from the pavement.

He watched Kimber throw a look towards the incoming goons, then back to him. "I can't," she said.

"Yes you can. Just run." He pointed down Desperation Avenue. "You're only four blocks away from the club. The boss will get you back."

There were more shots now. Just the goons trying to clear the crowds that had gathered around the intersection. Takashi could read indecision in Kimber's eyes.

"You kept me alive all night," she whispered. "I can't just leave you here."

Takashi shook his head. "You're not leaving me here. I'm telling you to go. So do it."

She gave him one last look, then turned and ran down the street.

Takashi waited until she was out of sight before he raised the pulse-pistol and pointed it towards the approaching goon squad. He wasn't going to be taken and tortured for information he didn't have. He was simply an employee, nothing more. But he wasn't going to give up his boss or … his girlfriend, either. Or Severen, who in a strange way had been his friend. No, they would have to kill him.

He waited until the first goon appeared, pushing his way through the crowd. Takashi took aim and blew the top of his blond head off, splattering skull and brain onto the crowds and the other goons. He found he had a smile on his face at this. Then he laughed out loud. He was already starting to fade away, and when he realized that, he was not surprised to find that it didn't bother him.

One of the remaining two goons raised his own pulse-pistol and ended Takashi's life with a single three-round burst, destroying the Japanese man's head.

~~~

Kimber did as Takashi had instructed, continuing down the street at a run. She dodged around a group of cyberpunks and made her way into the street. She slid the blinking device into one ear. She didn't like the way it passed so easily into her. It was too much like the violations she had already suffered. "Hello?" she asked, hesitant. She didn't stop running as she moved around a stopped cab.

"Kimber?" It was that voice, *his* voice. He was still there.

"Yes. Takashi is … dead. I'm alone. What do I do?"

"Where are you?" The voice had become like steel.

"I'm on Desperation Avenue. Takashi said I was only four blocks—"

"And you'll follow that all the way here, then you—"

"But those men are still behind me. Takashi may have killed one, I heard a lot of shots just now—"

"Then stop talking to me and get a move on," Spider growled. "Bring them right to me. I'm waiting. Four blocks."

"But—"

"Trust me, Kimber. I'll get you here."

Kimber was about to answer him when a burst of gunfire from behind caused her to cry out and duck behind a car. She kept moving, dodging between cars and cabs and whatever else was in her way.

~~~

"Thrash, you still on the line?" Spider asked, knowing that she would respond.

"I'm here."

"Did you get all that?"

"Yes." Her response was empty, hollow. He knew that he should say something to her. She and Takashi had grown quite close in the last few months. She had taken to caring for his ailing grandmother when he was working other jobs. They had been thinking about getting a place together, at least that was what he had heard. But the words just wouldn't come.

Finally, Thrash said, "I'll go get him later, boss. Bring him back. His grandmother would want that."

"I'll go with you. Until then, stay focused."

"I am, boss."

Spider felt the black hole in his heart grow larger. "He was a good man, Thrash."

"Later, boss. You need to stay focused as well."

She was right, he knew that. He shook it off as best he could and adjusted the rifle once more. He wanted to tell her that he was sorry, those were the words that he wanted to use that refused to come. But he couldn't.

~~~

Kimber climbed over the roof of a cab, not caring when the driver screamed at her in Mandarin. She could understand him perfectly. She would've responded to his rude insult if she'd had the time, but she ignored him and kept moving.

A look over her shoulder told her that the men in suits were now about thirty feet behind her and closing fast. There were only two of them left. Takashi must've got one before they … She pushed the thought away and focused on her feet as they rose and fell on the pavement. People were turning to stare at her now, but she didn't care.

She got back onto the sidewalk and pushed her way through a crowd of people standing outside a bar, all smoking cheap cigarettes. Kimber moved through their clouds of smoke and waved a hand in front of her face. But she didn't stop. She was spun around by a woman with long purple braids and dark eyeglasses who swore at her in Russian and jabbed a finger into her chest. Kimber shoved the woman aside and kept going, blocking out the shouts of the woman's compatriots.

She crossed another intersection, counting it in her mind. Three more to go. The corner was filled with people, so she bypassed it and ran through the street once more, telling herself that she could make it. This time, the gunshots behind her did not make her scream. In fact, she didn't make a sound, she just kept moving.

She chanced a look behind her as she passed a JR Cab, peering through the back window at the street. She could see the two men in suits approaching the intersection one block behind her. They were getting closer, she knew it. Kimber stood up and got off the street, pushing and being pushed in return as she made her way onto the crowded sidewalk. No one gave her any attitude this time, and she was grateful for that much at least.

She didn't slow down as she moved through the people, keeping herself as low as possible. With all the people around her, she thought it would be easier to hide from the men in the suits. So she bent low at the knees and skirted groups of people to stay out of sight. She followed along beside a Valmont Vertiijo, keeping herself below window level and shuffling her feet as the car inched slowly forward. Then she stood up quickly and kept moving, dismissing the stares from the young couple inside the car.

Kimber tripped on a pothole and stumbled for only a moment before she kept going.

The neon signs and the strangely-dressed people and the smells of the place all pushed in on her as she crossed yet another intersection. Two left, she told herself. From here, crossing the street, she could see the final intersection ahead of her. She didn't have the energy to smile. All of it was being devoted to escape.

She heard a scuffle behind her, but she didn't bother to turn around. The scuffle was followed by gunshots and grunts of pain. The suits must've run into some trouble on the sidewalk. She could hear screams joining in the grunts of pain, but she ignored this as well. Nothing she could do, as cold as it sounded in her own mind. She had her own problems to deal with.

Kimber reached the final intersection, which was clogged with traffic. Desperation was at a stand-still as traffic flowed down this road, which was called Dameron Street according to the sign above her head. Kimber ignored the shouts as she climbed over the hood of a cab, giving the driver the finger as he told her to shove a broken bottle up her cunt. She wanted to do more, but she didn't have the time. She found that all the anger, all the undirected rage she had felt during this entire ordeal and the events that preceded it, was flowing right through her, begging to be set loose on someone, anyone. But she kept it in check. There would be time for that later, if she lived long enough.

Her feet splashed into a puddle of filthy rain water as she ran down the street. She avoided the sidewalks now. It was easier to move through the stopped cars and traffic than it was to push and shove her way through the crowds. The stares and looks she received didn't bother her one bit.

More gunfire behind her, and several rounds ricocheted off the cab she had just climbed over. Another burst, and she could feel bullets whizzing through the air past her face and hair. They were getting closer. She didn't know how close, and she didn't want to stop and find out, so she kept moving. Across the street, she returned to a flat-out run and spoke into the ear piece. "I just crossed Dameron Street. What now?"

"Next intersection is Colton Street. Turn left and follow it to an alley on your right. Alley will lead you behind the club and the Hive. On your right will be a second alley with a black arrow pointing up it. Take the alley. It'll lead you right to me."

"What about them?"

"They want you and that implant. They'll follow."

"Are you sure?"

"I told you to trust me, Kimber."

"Okay." She didn't stop as she reached the final intersection, the one Spider had called Colton Street. And there, above her head, was the street sign. She moved on, crossing into the street despite the traffic. She was nearly hit by a young punkish couple in an old Montressor, but she sidestepped the car's bumper and kept moving.

She moved down Colton Street towards the alley, trying to keep it in sight through the crowds of people moving up and down the sidewalk. Here, no one gave her a second look. She was just another face in the sea of faces. As she approached the alley on her right, she heard shouts from the street corner followed by a scream. Kimber took a moment to glance behind her as she ducked into the alley, and she could see the two men in suits, waving their weapons in the air and moving towards her. One of them fired in her direction, the rounds striking the building on her right and sending chips of mortar flying towards her. She didn't stick around to see any more than that.

Kimber pumped her arms as she ran down the alley, being careful not to slip in the piles of rotting garbage that filled the alley's floor. A pair of rats ambled out of her way as she stepped over them, disappearing behind an overflowing garbage can. A cat leapt from a darkened corner and dashed across her path after the rats, hissing at her as it passed. She ignored it and kept moving.

The second alley, the one that would lead her to Spider, opened up on her right, just like he said it would. More filth and garbage met her, along with the sour-sweet smell of decay. She climbed over a tumbled stack of cardboard boxes, slipping and falling but fighting her way to the top once more. Behind her, she could hear the two men in suits as they shouted back and forth to each other. They were telling each other where she had gone, that much she could glean from their conversation. Kimber forced their voices out of her mind and kept moving.

~~~

Spider could hear Kimber moving down the alley. At least, he hoped it was Kimber. All he could tell from the shifting of boxes and the patter of feet on asphalt was that *someone* was coming down the alley. He shifted his crouch slightly and readjusted the rifle for what felt like the hundredth time.

Below, he could see shadows moving down the alley in the club's meager spotlight. Whoever it was, they were heading straight for him. Spider glared through the scope, keeping the crosshairs on the center of the alley. When Kimber appeared, he nearly shot her.

"Are you alright?" he spoke into his own ear piece.

"Yes. Where do—"

"There's a door on your right. Pound on it twice with your fist and it should open." Spider kept his eye on the alley, not concerned with Kimber at the moment. He heard her fist hit the door, twice as instructed, at the same moment that he saw the first suited goon creep into the alley. He wanted to fire, but he needed them both in the alley before he could do that. He waited as the goon moved up, silently willing the second goon to appear as well.

"The door isn't opening," he heard Kimber whisper in his ear.

"Be quiet," he hissed. *Come on*, he shouted inside his head. *Give me something to shoot. Come on.* The first goon was nearly to the center of the alley, where it would open up and allow him to see Kimber. Spider cursed inside his head and pulled the trigger. He had no choice now.

The first goon went down in a spray of blood as the DM-8's .450 magnum round obliterated his neck, popping his head off his shoulders. Spider shot him a second time just to be sure. Kimber dropped to the ground and covered her head. Spider raised the rifle and aimed down the alley, waiting for the second goon to show himself.

While still on the ground, Kimber beat against the door with one fist, not bothering to space her knocks anymore. There was a frantic look on her face that Spider recognized. He had seen it on the faces of people running down Desperation Avenue late at night, and he had seen it on the faces of girls led up to this very roof by Quartez's so-called clients. He tried not to think about it as he gazed through the scope.

The second goon finally showed himself, peeking around the alley's far corner. Spider lined up the shot and waited, hoping that the goon would simply stroll around and give him a clean shot but knowing it wouldn't happen. He hoped anyway.

Below him, he could still hear Kimber banging on the door.

The second goon shot out from the alley's corner and dove behind a group of trash cans, firing his pulse-pistol at the roof. Spider wasn't concerned about the man's rounds as they bounced off the masonry below him. He knew the goon couldn't see him and did not know where the first two shots had come from. Spider adjusted the rifle, giving the goon some space this time.

The goon finally made his move, firing his weapon at random towards the roof and running for another grouping of refuse and garbage cans about ten yards up the alley. Spider waited two seconds and fired, catching the goon in the left shoulder and blowing most of his left arm off. The goon screamed and Spider raised the rifle, bringing the crosshairs to rest on the man's forehead as he dropped to the ground. Spider pulled the trigger and the goon's head disappeared in a spray of blood and brain matter, coating the alley's walls behind him.

Spider lowered the rifle and stood up, watching the rain as it began to rinse the dead men's blood and matter down hidden drains. His eyes found Kimber, now on her feet by the door and looking right at him. Her eyes seemed to burn through his body. She spoke, and he could hear her voice inside his ear. "Thanks." Her voice was hard, but he could detect sadness behind it. It was a sadness that he felt as well.

"You're welcome." He looked away. "Thrash? Send Severen to get that fucking door open now. And find out why nobody was waiting to open it. Have him bring Kimber back to the Hive. Find me Satoshi or Dauphine, whichever one answers first, and have her meet me on the second floor. Then call Finnegan and get him out here to clean up these bodies. Make sure he gets some drink tickets for the bar. When Severen gets back with the girl, send him back out here to take some pictures of these assholes. They're the only ones we haven't ID'd yet. I've got a good idea who they are, though." He looked back at Kimber. "Stay right there. Somebody's gonna open the door in a minute."

She nodded. "Okay."

"I'll stay here until they do." He heard the Hive's door open and turned his head to watch Severen cross the catwalk in the rain, punching in his own code and disappearing into the club. A minute later, and the door below swung open. Severen was there, holding out one hand. "Come on," he said, and Kimber stepped through the opening. Severen gave Spider a look from the doorway, then pulled the door closed behind him.

Spider took a deep breath. What a fucking night.

10

QUARTEZ MET HIM as he came out of the stairway, closing the door behind him and still holding the rifle in one hand. Her eyes were wide with panic, but as she saw the look on his own face, that panic seemed to ease itself.

"What the hell is going on?" she asked, not demanding but pleading. "The girls have been on high alert for—"

"Everything's fine, Diana. I took care of it."

"That girl from before, I just saw Severen leading her up from the—"

"Why wasn't anyone on the door?"

"We heard shots in the alley way and locked it tight. Usual protocol. I didn't know it was you."

"Now you do. Don't do that again." Spider turned away from her and began to walk towards the main staircase. Quartez dropped a hand onto his shoulder, stopping him in his tracks.

"Is it true?" she asked. "Did Takashi … is he dead?"

Spider nodded. "Yes." He swept her hand off his shoulder and continued on.

"I'm sorry, Spider," she called after him, but he waved her off as he took the stairs to the second floor.

When he reached the bottom, he found Satoshi waiting for him. "You wanted to see me?" She was leaning against the stairway's rail, her black cocktail dress showing off her legs.

Satoshi

"I need to borrow you for an hour or so."

She chuckled. "Aw, Spider, I was wondering when you'd get around to me."

He shook his head. "Not like that, Tosh. I need you for a job. How'd you like to not take your clothes off for sweaty men for the next hour or two?"

"Sounds good to me. What's up?"

"Change your clothes and meet me at my table in ten minutes. Wear something more professional."

"I don't own any suits, Spider. Sorry."

"Don't be a smart ass. Ten minutes." He walked past her, his eye turning involuntarily to the stage. The Grenade Sisters, Jane and Stana, were busy breathing fire at one another. Spider had never seen this act before, and a part of him wondered absently when they had decided to try it out. He hadn't seen any rehearsals or—

The image of Takashi as he had been earlier in the evening, with his suit and his glass of Chivas, entered his mind, and all other thoughts disappeared. Takashi had been a good man, and a good ... *friend* was the word Spider was looking for. In a place like this, friends were a luxury that most people didn't have. But Takashi had been his.

Spider turned away from the stage as he reached the door, the Grenade Sisters instantly leaving his mind. He punched in his code and left the club behind, stepping into the rain once more. The two bodies were still in the alley, their blood rinsing down drains. And there, by the door, he could see Marisol and Ariana, huddled together underneath the tiny awning. Marisol waved at him, but he didn't return it. Instead, he crossed the catwalk to the Hive's entrance and punched in his code, not even thinking about it.

The building was silent when he walked in. From up here, he could see Thrash and Severen, both at their consoles and trying hard to avoid looking at him or each other. Kimber was nowhere to be seen, but he figured she was just below him, laying or sitting on the ratty old couch that was so comfortable. As he came down the spiral staircase, he caught a glimpse of her, exactly where he thought she would be, with her head resting on the couch's arm.

Spider set the DM-8 down, leaning it against the Hive's wall. "Did you get the pictures?" he asked, directing the question in Severen's direction.

The other man nodded. "Yeah. I'm running them now."

"Good." Spider crossed the room to Thrash's console, forcing his mouth to form the words. He laid one hand on her shoulder. "I'm sorry," he managed, the words feeling awkward from his own mouth.

Thrash just nodded, not meeting his gaze.

"We'll go get him when this is over. If not, I can have Finnegan bring him back here."

Another nod.

"Then we'll go see his grandmother together, okay?"

"Yes." The word was empty. Spider forced the ice to flow through his veins once more. He took his hand off her shoulder and turned around.

Kimber was laying on the couch, her eyes glued to him. She was soaked to the bone, but she didn't seem to care. He crossed the area and kneeled down in front of her, meeting her eyes with his own. What he saw there … it brought fear into his heart. He pushed it away and spoke to her. "We need to get you into some dry clothes. And probably some fresh bandages as well."

Kimber nodded and dropped her eyes. "I didn't want him to die for me."

Spider was struck dumb by the honesty of her words, and the courage it must've taken for her to say them. When she brought her eyes back to meet his gaze, he could see a strength there that he hadn't known she possessed. Maybe she hadn't known it either, before tonight. But she did now. He could see it. "Nobody wanted it. But it happened. Get changed so we can finish this. Last thing you need is to get sick right now. Come on." He offered her his hand, and she took it. He led her back to the living quarters, pointing towards a bank of lockers tucked in the rear. "There's some extra clothes in there that should fit you. I'm gonna dry off a little and change as well. Be back out there in five." He pointed to the main area of the Hive, then turned away and headed for his private room.

Five minutes later, Spider was dressed in a black Ven Evers suit with dry hair and clean socks. He came out of his room and made his way through the living quarters to the main area, where he found Kimber sitting on the couch, now dressed in a green T-shirt and a pair of jeans. She had a light rain jacket folded across her knees, and her hands were resting on it, folded primly.

"What do we have on the goon squad?" Spider asked his tech monkeys, not caring who answered him. He didn't take his eyes off Kimber, and her own gaze never left his.

"Anthony Dunn and Scott Pillser," answered Severen. "Dunn is a Sagittarius who owns a small townhome in the Green District, while Pillser is a Capricorn who enjoys long walks on the beach and—"

"Not in the mood," Spider hissed. "Give me the details straight up."

"They're Flynn International goons, boss," Thrash interjected. "Their employment files say they both work private security for the company, riding in cars with VIPs and following the executives around the city. Flynn has an office here, in case you didn't know, deep in the Yellow District. Second tallest building in the city."

Flynn? Spider was taken aback. Why would Flynn International be after the girl? Before he could finish that thought, the answer hit him: the implant. They wanted the implant, same as everyone else. Everything that had happened tonight, including Takashi's death, had been about that goddamn piece of metal. He crossed the Hive to Severen's workstation, where the plastic tube containing the implant rested. He picked it up and eyed the device within. So small. So useless now. He set it down. "How long will it take to find God?"

Thrash sighed deeply. "She's buried pretty deep, boss. It's not like picking up the phone and calling your mom. Could take some time."

"Find her. Get me a line."

"What are you gonna do in the meantime?"

Spider turned away from her to face Kimber. "Get a drink. I need it. So does she." He indicated Kimber with one finger. "Call me when you find her. We're supposed to check in once the assignment's completed."

"On it, boss," said Thrash, and dropped her eyes back to the console.

Spider offered Kimber his hand, and she took it, slipping her jacket on as she stood up. She moved towards the spiral staircase ahead of him, and he let her. His mind focused once more on Takashi. He hadn't realized until a few minutes ago just how much he would miss the man. He was cold, to be sure, and distant, but he had been someone that Spider could count on, and that made him a friend. Trust was a rare commodity in the Red. It was hard sometimes to tell what another person's true motivation was.

At the top of the stairs, Spider turned his gaze to the Hive, taking in his two employees, their consoles, and all the equipment beyond them. His own little operation. He turned away from it and opened the door, holding it for Kimber as she slipped past him and into the rain. Drops rolled off her jacket and spattered the catwalk as she moved to the second door and waited. Spider found his eyes drawn to hers, and when he tried to break the contact, he found that he couldn't. What was it about this girl? Why was she in his head?

He punched in his code and swung the door open, once again holding it for Kimber.

The atmosphere was as he had left it. Nothing was out of place. The girls could get ready for a fight and perform at the same time. The show had to go on, of course. Vinyssa was performing her signature hoop act on the stage, smiling and winking at customers. Spider and Kimber crossed the VIP area to his table, and Marisol was already there with his bottle and a clean glass. "Bring me another," he said, pointing to the glass. Marisol disappeared for a moment, then set another glass on the table.

Spider dropped into his seat and poured himself a drink. He gulped it down in two swallows, then poured another. "6 Underground" filled Spider's ears as he took a sip of his drink. His eyes found Vinyssa on the stage once more. She was finishing up now, and that meant that Ariana and what would normally be Satoshi were preparing for one of the night's "Finale" shows, meant to remind the audience that the club was winding down and the shift change would happen soon. He wondered who Quartez would shanghai into filling in for the Japanese girl now that he had drafted her into his service for the night. He found the thought strange. Satoshi and Dauphine were the only people in the club who he both trusted and had the necessary bodyguard experience to do the job. If this worked out, Satoshi might never take her clothes off again.

Vinyssa gathered her hoops from the stage floor and scampered off to stage left as Marisol returned with a clean glass. She set it in front of Spider, who filled it with

Chivas as the Hispanic girl moved away. Then he slid the glass across the table to Kimber. When she didn't pick it up, he pushed the glass closer to her. "Drink it," he said. "It'll help."

Kimber took the glass and stared at the amber liquid inside, swishing it back and forth against the glass's sides. Then she drank it down.

"Better?"

Kimber nodded but did not speak. She sipped the drink again, swallowing half of it in one gulp.

Spider let his gaze drift over the stage. Ariana and Meridian, who did not look happy, ambled across the stage, both dressed in matching catsuits with belled collars. He could barely hear the tinkling of the bells over the pumping dance music that suddenly filled the club. He turned away and sipped his drink.

"What will happen to me now?"

Spider met her own eyes with his, and found genuine concern there. She really had no idea. If he was honest, he didn't, either. "I don't know. We have to talk to God first. She'll have an idea."

"Why do you call her that name?"

Now Spider found he had a ghost of a smile on his face. "Because she sees all and knows all. She can go anywhere on the 'Net that she wants to. Because nothing is off-limits or out-of-reach for her. She's everywhere at once, and she's nowhere at the same time. I don't even know where she is."

Kimber nodded, but did not speak. Her own eyes moved to the stage, watching the girls move about. Ariana had a bull whip in one hand now, and was slowly unfurling it to the crowd's delight. The look of surprise on Meridian's face seemed to be genuine. If it wasn't, Spider thought to himself, then maybe she should take over the show from Satoshi.

And speaking of which, he thought, as Satoshi crested the stairs and made her way to his table. She was now dressed completely in black; heels, blouse, loose pants that allowed freer movement of her legs. She had even pulled her hair back in a ponytail, which he had never seen her do. That hair of hers was one of the things clients seemed to love about her. "Am I interrupting something?" she asked, her gaze flicking from Spider to Kimber and back again.

Spider shook his head and indicated the seat next to Kimber. "No. Sit." Once she had positioned herself in the chair, Spider took another sip of his drink. "I need you working security tonight," he began. "With Tak … gone, I need somebody next to me. Somebody I can trust. Besides Dauphine, you're the only one in this place with any training. And considering everything that's happened tonight, I think I need that."

"What *has* happened tonight, Spider?" Satoshi's voice was low, just above a whisper.

"You'll find out soon enough. A lot of things are going to change pretty quick, Tosh. Just be ready. If it goes well, you might not be going back to stripping." Satoshi's face lit up at those words, but she kept it in check. *Always the coolest one in the room*, thought Spider. He took another sip of his Chivas. "Just stick to me like glue and we'll get through this, okay? And don't worry, you'll get paid for it."

Satoshi nodded, but said nothing.

"You're going to see some things. Things you may not be able to explain, and things that you certainly can't talk about. Okay? I'm serious here."

Satoshi seemed to study him for a moment before she responded. "You can trust me, Spider."

"I already do. Don't make me regret it." Then he turned his eyes to Kimber. "This will be over soon. I promise." He felt stupid saying it out loud, but it was what he felt. He'd never been one to speak his feelings, but here it was. He wanted her out of this. He wanted something better for her, and he felt like an idiot for admitting it to himself. What the hell did he know about her, other than the fact that she was … an abductee? That in and of itself was not enough to make him … but was it? Because that seemed to be the way his head and heart were moving.

Kimber said nothing. She simply sipped her drink and continued to stare back at him.

Spider was grateful when his phone rang a few minutes later, as the silence was driving him crazy. Even in a place like this, where music played almost constantly, the silences could still get in your head and make you uncomfortable. He pulled the smartphone from his pocket and swiped a finger across the face before bringing it to his ear. "Yeah?"

It was Severen. "Thrash thinks she may have found God, but it's iffy."

"We're on the way." He hung up the phone and dropped it into his jacket pocket. "We've got a meeting with God." He stood up and buttoned his jacket.

Satoshi brought up the rear as the group moved across the second floor to Spider's steel door. They waited while Spider entered his code. Kimber went first, followed by Spider. Again, Satoshi brought up the rear, closing the door behind them and following them to the second door. She looked down at the alley and noticed the two bodies still lying there, but she said nothing.

Satoshi followed them through the second door, her eyes taking in the Hive for the first time. She had never been here before, never even knew what was behind the door. She knew about the catwalk, but never where it led. Spider kept his business to himself; other than knowing that he rented the Hive from Quartez and the name of the building itself, she had no idea what went on here. Now she was beginning to see.

As the three took the spiral staircase to the first floor, Satoshi asked, "So what exactly is it that you do here, Spider?"

"Bake cookies," Spider retorted, but then he turned to her and flashed her a soft look, as if he was apologizing for the venom in his reply. "You'll see soon enough. But there are formalities to follow." At the bottom of the staircase, Spider called out, "What's the good word?"

"Nothing yet," Severen replied. Spider could see that Thrash was buried in her own console at the moment, doing God knew what.

"Hurry up." He said nothing more, but his patience was wearing thin. God treated him as her own employee, when in fact he was not. He simply did her favors once in a while. But, he thought, that once in a while shit was happening far too often now, especially as far as the … His brain was doing it again, forcing that word out his mind before he could even give it space. But he wouldn't let it, not anymore. Things had changed tonight. They were abductees. What happened to them was real. The proof was standing right next to him.

He glanced down at the plastic tube he held in his right hand. The device held within seemed so small, so useless. What was the point of killing over something smaller than a nail clipping? Something that didn't even work now? He knew the reasons, he just didn't see the point. Spider shook his head and turned back to Severen. "What exactly is the hold-up here?"

Severen shook his head and did not answer.

~~~

The balcony was on the apartment building's fifty-seventh floor, high above the streets of Shinjuku, Tokyo. The city's noise and neon did not reach this high, but the balcony offered an unparalleled view of the city, even at four o'clock in the afternoon. Directly across the street was Shinjuku Station, the city's largest rail terminal, bathed in afternoon sunlight. Below, the city went about its business. Horns honked, buses weaved through traffic, a lone policeman stood beneath a traffic light doing a thankless job.

But here, on the fifty-seventh floor, the balcony was an island, a lone entity. There was nothing else. Only the balcony existed. And on this balcony, in a classic lotus position, sat the Cyber Princess.

Her red hair was pulled back into a tight ponytail, and her eyes were closed. She breathed in and out in a slow rhythm. The pink T-shirt she wore, the one that read *SuperGenius* across the front, rose and fell with each deep breath. Her hands, palms up, rested on her knees, and the flannel of her pajama pants flapped in the slight breeze around her. Her bare feet were tucked beneath her, mostly to keep them warm.

Elizabeth Wilder aka God

Her mind was an empty vessel; no trace of self remained. All thought was banished, unwelcome. The concept of herself, of ego, was gone. There was only blackness, a sense of … of no-self. Her heartbeat had slowed itself to a crawl. The technique had been easy to learn, at least for her, but the result? She had spent the last three years working toward that goal. Only a few weeks ago had she finally mastered it.

It took ten minutes to bring herself up from this trance-like state.

When she was finished, she opened her eyes and surveyed the Tokyo skyline around her. Far off to her right, she could see the lights of Kabukicho, the city's red-light district. The action never stopped there, she knew. To her left, she could see the Skyscraper District, so named because it held the city's first constructed skyscraper. Additionally, the district held the Tokyo Metropolitan Government Building as well as many of the city's in-demand hotels such as the Keio Plaza and the Park Hyatt. Lights were on in many of the offices and she knew that many of them would be on for another three to four hours. The Japanese were notorious for their long work-weeks.

The Cyber Princess stood up and looked over the balcony's rail. Below her, she could see pedestrians scrambling into Shinjuku Station to make a train or crossing the street from the station to get somewhere important known only to them. She shook her head and turned away, reaching for a door handle. The glass door slid open and she stepped inside.

The apartment was meager, containing only what she needed. Most of it was reserved for her work. The rest was crammed against a wall. A small kitchen in one corner contained a tea kettle that was whistling loudly. The Cyber Princess crossed the apartment, stepping over cables wound together with electrical tape and coils of fiber-optic wire. She turned her head slightly to the right as she approached the kitchen and said, "Television control: give me news channels fifteen hundred through fifteen hundred forty five in a five-second scroll. Focus on tech stories and politics. Show me Nikkai Index, and display Nasdaq and New York Stock Exchange in a scroll below as soon as each one opens for the day." There was a resounding beep that echoed through the small apartment, then a bank of flat-screen televisions, each a different size, switched on to her right, blazing light into the dark abode. The sound of multiple talking heads pushed out the apartment's silence, replacing it with an endless cycle of news. The Cyber Princess lifted her tea kettle off the stove and switched the infrared burner off. She moved to her left and poured the boiling water into a small blue ceramic cup. The kettle went back onto the burner, and the Cyber Princess stirred the mixture with a spoon.

She carried the mug across the apartment to the bank of computers and servers that took up most of the space. Here, she sat down behind a desk which contained three monitors and a large digital camera aimed at her own face. She switched the machines on, smiling as everything began to hum and whir with the power that flowed through it. While she waited for her gear to boot up, she glanced at the televisions, searching each one for anything that caught her eye. When nothing did, she turned back to her computers.

The noise of the talking heads became overwhelming in its own way, until she couldn't stand it any longer. "Television control: mute." Instantly, the sounds were gone. The Cyber Princess smiled and began typing on a nearby keyboard. Then she said, "Stereo control: give me Stray Cats. Random play. Repeat all." The smile became a grin as "Stray Cat Strut" began to thump through the speakers hidden within the apartment. She bounced back and forth for several moments as she tapped away on her keyboard.

It took a few more minutes for her to realize that someone wanted to talk to her. Using back-channels and ghost IP addresses, she finally discovered that Spider's team had been trying to find her for the last twenty

CARTER JOHNSON

minutes. She had been deeper into her meditation than she must've thought. She found a secure connection and piggy-backed on it all the way to the Hive.

The Cyber Princess tapped several keys, turning the camera on and adjusting the view. Then she waited.

~~~

Spider grunted in frustration and turned back to Severen. "So? Is she online or what?"

Severen nodded. "She's coming, boss." A few moments, then Severen began to type on his keyboard. He pointed to the main screen. "All yours."

Spider uncrossed his arms and waited while the screen flashed a brief burst of static, then the face of God resolved itself from the pixels. Her hair had been pulled back, and she had changed her clothes. He hated that T-shirt she was wearing. There was a blue mug in her right hand that he assumed was filled with tea of some kind.

"What's up, Spider? All done?"

"All done, my ass. You owe me more than money for this one. I lost my best man tonight."

God was silent for several moments before she said, "I'm sorry, Spider. Really."

Spider glared at her. "It's gonna take more than that to make this right. He was … my friend."

God, not one to back down easily, returned his glare, then shifted her eyes to the form leaning against the wall behind Spider. "Who's that?"

Spider turned his head, caught Satoshi out of the corner of his eye. He turned back to the screen. "That's my new bodyguard. At least for the time being. I trust her."

"Well, no offense, but I don't. I don't even know her."

"You didn't know Takashi, either."

"All things being equal, Spider, I'm going to run a background on her before I say another word, got it?"

"Do your thing. We can wait." He had known that something like this might happen. God's paranoia was, in many ways, understandable. She had governments the world over looking for her, not to mention whatever other enemies she had made along the way. Someone like God didn't get where she was without pissing people off.

God punched several keys on her end of the line while Spider crossed his arms and waited. No one spoke as God worked. Even the tech monkeys were silent. Spider knew they both regarded God as, well, a god. To them, she was the Ultimate, the Supreme. She knew more and had done more than almost any other single person in the world. If she died tomorrow, the entire world's population of hackers would mourn her, in their own ways.

Finally, God looked up and met his gaze. "She's clean."

"I already told you that."

God ignored his comment for the time being, turning her attention to Kimber. "Are you alright, Jennifer?"

Kimber nodded. "I wanted it out, and now it is."

God smiled. "Yes it is." Back to Spider. "Did you get it?"

Spider held up the plastic container. "Yes. Just like you asked."

"Good. Now tell me what happened."

"Some Flynn International goons ambushed Takashi and … Jennifer as they were leaving the Doc's place a few blocks from here. Jennifer took a round in the shoulder and we needed to get her patched up before she bled out in the street, so Tak took her there. He said that four suits were in the hallway after he came out of the room with her. When he tried to get her back here, they killed him. We got photos of two of them and Severen was able to trace them back to Flynn International. So they want the implant also. Right?"

God waited a moment before she answered. "Yes. Governments aren't the only ones after it. All the private corps want it too, mostly for the science." She took a deep breath. "Again, I'm sorry that your man was killed, Spider. This is a dirty business. Sometimes it happens."

Spider shook his head and chuckled, but there was no humor behind it. He couldn't believe her right now. His man had just been killed and that was the best she could come up with? Wasn't she supposed to be smart? He pushed it out of his mind for now. He had bigger things on his plate. "So what's the plan, Queenie? Are we sending her down the line?"

God shook her head. "You just have to have a nickname for me, don't you? Can't ever let it go." She punched several keys on her keyboard. "Maybe I'll drop that FBI file anyway."

"Fine. Cyber."

"Thank you. Now, I've got some calls to make, but yes, I think we should send her on. She needs help, more than what we can do for her." God's eyes flicked to the girl, and Spider could see genuine compassion in the super-hacker's eyes. It had been a long time since he had felt that emotion, but if he was honest with himself, he was feeling it right now too. Spider found himself looking at the girl next to him differently. She wasn't a refugee, she wasn't an abductee ... she was a person. She had dreams and fears and doubts and hopes and maybe a family somewhere that was worried about her and ... He looked away, fighting back a show of emotion that would damage his reputation. It took everything he had. Instead, he turned his gaze to God, whose eyes seemed to reflect the pain he felt within himself. There was a hint of a smile in one corner of her mouth.

Spider took a moment to compose himself, then asked, "Where will she go?"

God wasn't expecting this question, at least from him. She hid the shock from her face, but not her eyes. Spider knew what she thought of him, knew what most thought of him. But he couldn't … they were people. They always had been. He simply had not let that idea seep into his brain. It made it easier to pass them on, or to not feel guilty if they died on the way. And now … Tak had died trying to keep this girl alive. He couldn't ignore that, either.

"I'm going to make a call, but I know some people who can help her. It's important that she get some kind of support for this, whether it be—"

"That's not what I asked." Spider found the words were rolling off his tongue before he had given them any thought. "I asked you where she's going."

Now God seemed to take pity on him. "Are you worried about her, Spider? That's not really your style, is it?"

"No it isn't. Just answer the question."

The Hive had become nearly silent when his question had been spoken. Now, it seemed even more so. He could've heard a pin drop in that silence. God looked at him with a serious eye for a moment before she answered. "There's a transporter who works out of Green District named Smith. He'll take her where she needs to go."

"And where exactly is that?"

God shook her head. "You know I can't tell you that, Spider, especially after what happened to Trace. We compartmentalize this operation to keep everyone safe." She cleared her throat. "You don't need to know."

"My man died to get that thing out of her arm and get her back here safely. *She* almost died for the same reason. They were chased through the city and my … friend … was killed for something that nobody really understands. Not to mention whatever God-awful shit *she's* already been through before she got here. And then there's … whatever happened to her in order for this fucking thing—" He shook the plastic container and watched God's eyes widen as the implant bounced back and forth within. "—to get inside her in the first place. So yeah, I think I need to know. Now." He held the implant as close to the small camera just below the screen as he could get it. "You want this? Tell me what happens next."

"Are you threatening me, Spider?" Her voice had gone cold and hard.

Before Spider could retort, Kimber spoke up, her voice tinged with what could've been hope. "Where am I going? Please."

God's face softened, as did Spider's. The two seemed to realize they were about to go to war over the fate of one girl. And that girl was not some thing. She had concerns of her own. Both parties seemed to have forgotten that.

Spider looked at Kimber and tried not to reach his hand out to touch her, to comfort her, to do anything that would make her realize that even with all the bad in the world, there was still some good left. But he didn't. He wanted to, but he didn't. She wasn't sticking around, he knew that, but still. The thought was there anyway. Maybe it was because he wasn't sure if he himself felt that anymore, that there was hope left in the world. He told himself it was simply because she was leaving.

God's tone, when she spoke, had become soft and gentle. "I'm going to put in a call to Smith. There are others I can call as well, if Smith isn't available for some reason. Either way, someone will pick you up from the club. Maybe around dawn, but maybe sooner. Just depends."

"Then what?" Kimber asked. She stared at God on the big screen, her face a blank slate, her eyes empty of emotion. "Where will he take me?"

Again, that voice was soft and gentle. "There is a man in the Green District named Rechter." She grunted. "I shouldn't have told you his name, secured line be damned. He's an ufologist and an investigator. He also has more contacts inside Millennium City than I could hope for. He knows psychologists, leaders of support groups, medical doctors, everything you could possibly need to get back on your feet. And you will get back on your feet. This is not going to be the rest of your life. I promise."

Spider had never heard God promise anything to anybody, let alone a random abductee. The word seemed easier to use now that he had accepted the ramifications. She wasn't a refugee, and it was time he put that term to rest. He wasn't sure if he could ever look at them, any of them, like that again.

God turned away from them and punched a few keys, then looked back. "I'll get back to you in a few minutes after I make these calls." She punched another button on her keyboard and the transmission ended.

Spider found himself turning his eye to the girl standing next to him. Kimber clasped her hands in front of her. Spider wondered if this wasn't a nervous habit, since he had seen her doing it many times tonight. It seemed impossible for her to relax, but given what she had been through, not just tonight but many others nights

CARTER JOHNSON

as well, he understood it. In her own way, Kimber was stronger than he would ever be. He couldn't imagine going through what she had and surviving it.

He badly wanted a cigarette. The tension in his body, still there from earlier, needed a release, and the nicotine would help with that. But he waited for the call instead. He knew it wouldn't be long, and then he could get that release, and he wouldn't have to worry about abductees that—

He cut the thought midway. *Don't go there*, he told himself. *Just let it go. She's leaving.* Spider closed his eyes for a moment and mentally pushed the thoughts out of his head. His finger twitched with need, but he held it in check.

God returned to the big screen a few minutes later. It was after three in the morning, according to Spider's watch. Her hair was loose now, spilling from her head and framing her face just so. She sipped her tea before she said, "I got ahold of Smith. He'll be there in twenty minutes." She turned her eye to Spider. "Think you can manage to keep her alive that long?"

Spider didn't answer right away. He wanted to shout profanity at her, wanted to release the rage he felt inside himself at the absurdity of the moment. Here he was, a known data thief and a convicted felon, smuggling alien abductees down a secret path to their final destinations of surgery, medication, and support groups that would be their lives. Him, Spider, the guy voted most likely to fuck up everything. And now, he was expending precious mental energy worrying about one of those abductees like … like she meant something to him.

But instead, he met her gaze and remained stoic. "Yeah, I think I can do that. Smith is taking her to this guy Rechter?"

"Yes. Don't use that name again. He will get her where she needs to go from here." Her stare turned to stone. "Stop asking me so many questions, Spider. This is the way it is for a reason, and you know that. I've already told you far more than you need to know. Just let it be."

Spider didn't speak, and after a few moments, God turned away and looked to Kimber. "You'll be in the car for about forty minutes, okay? Then this other man will get you settled for the night and you can get some sleep. From there, he'll know what to do. This is the last stop, okay? From here on out, you'll be on your own. There will be no further communication from me, understand?"

Kimber nodded. "Is he … nice? This man Rechter."

God didn't correct her like she did with Spider. "I wouldn't go that far, but he's decent enough. He'll take care of you and get you what you need."

Another nod. "Okay."

God looked at Spider. "Do me a favor and keep your eye on her until Smith gets there." A smile grew in one corner of her mouth. "I'll feel better knowing she's not running loose in the club."

This seemed to ease some of the tension between her and Spider. He found he had a ghost of a smile on his own face. "I'll do that." But as the tension flowed away, Spider found he was left with something else, something he didn't like. He turned to his left, where Satoshi was leaning against the wall like a statue, completely motionless. "Take her into the club, Tosh. I'll meet you at my table in a few minutes." The Japanese woman nodded. Kimber allowed herself to be gently led away, up the stairs and out the door.

When they were gone, Spider looked at his tech monkeys. "You two, take five. Hit the club for a while. You earned it tonight."

"What about the transmission?" Thrash asked.

"Yeah," Severen added, "someone needs to stay and monitor the—"

Spider turned his back to them, facing God once more. "I said, take five. Go get a drink and try to relax for a few. You're off the clock for now."

Severen jumped out of his seat. "You got it, boss." He was up the stairs and out the door without another word.

Thrash lagged behind. "You okay, boss?"

"Yeah. Go relax. I got this."

She tossed her headset onto the computer desk and turned around. "Don't have too much fun without us."

"I'll try not to."

When the door had eased shut behind her, the locks re-engaging automatically, Spider found himself alone with the image of God on a television screen above him. He didn't need to say anything. It was written all over his face.

"What's on your mind, Spider?" God asked. "You and I don't normally have one-on-one conversations."

Spider took several moments to answer. Holding back his emotions, he looked her in the eye and said, "I don't know if I can do this anymore."

"Do what?"

He swept a hand behind him. "This. These ... abductees. After tonight, I don't ... I can't look at them like refugees anymore. I can't watch these people go through this and not ... not care anymore. And I ... Takashi was my friend. I don't have many of those. And I lost him tonight."

God smiled at him. "You're growing a heart, Spider. It's not such a bad thing."

He shook his head. "Having a heart isn't good for business. You know that."

"Maybe. Or maybe it'll help."

"I don't see how."

"Best not to worry about it right now. You've got a job to do."

Another shake. "It's not just a job anymore. They're people."

"Like I said, a heart." She looked away for several moments, then began to type on her keyboard as she talked. "I'm going to wire the payment into your usual account, unless you say otherwise. You certainly earned it tonight." Then she turned back to him. Her eyes seemed to bore into him, seeing the parts he kept hidden. She managed to smile and scowl at him simultaneously. "I've got things to do, Spider. If you want that girl to stay, go tell her."

Spider was taken aback by her forwardness, and by her insight. "It's not that." He knew that was a lie even as he said it. "But she's got a name and probably a family and maybe friends who are worried about her, and—"

"So go tell her that."

After a moment of silence, Spider said, "I need a drink. Call me when you have some more work."

"You're not stepping out?"

"No." He sighed, dropping his eyes from the screen. "Keep sending them."

God smiled. "I'll do that. You take care of yourself, Spider. Even if you are an asshole." God tapped a key, and the transmission ended.

11

SPIDER TOOK A deep breath, then crossed the Hive to the living quarters. Hidden behind a bank of lockers was his private stash. He uncapped the bottle and took a long drink, then sat down on the edge of one of the cots nearby. He took another drink and tried not to think about the girl, but he couldn't help it. What would happen to her? Where would she go, after all this? Could she have a life after something so traumatic?

After a few minutes, Spider put the bottle away and checked his watch. It was after three-thirty now. The tech monkeys were back at their consoles, punching away at keys. Severen wore a three-shot grin on his face as Spider moved to the staircase. He left the Hive and walked into the club.

Ellegarta and Marisol were on stage, performing their dirty Kabuki routine. Spider tuned it out as he crossed the VIP area to his table. Satoshi and Kimber were already seated. The bottle of Chivas was back on the table, and each had a glass in front of them. Spider sat down in his regular seat and poured himself a glass. Then he reached into his jacket for his cigarettes, and lit one.

Kimber noticed, and she pointed to the pack as he slid it back into his jacket. "Can I have one of those?" she asked.

Spider nodded and handed the pack over. He used his own Zippo to light the cigarette for her, then deposited pack and lighter into the jacket's pocket.

Kimber took a long drag and closed her eyes.

Spider leaned forward and asked, "How are you doing? Are you okay with all of this?"

She blew smoke from her nose and looked at him through the cloud. "What if I wasn't?"

Spider didn't know what to say to that. Was it an invitation? He turned to his right and saw Bridgit still behind the bar, pouring a drink for herself. At this time of night, every bartender in the Red was doing the same thing. She downed the drink and looked over at him, flashing him a smile and a wink.

Back to Kimber. She took another drag and tapped ash into the large tray in the center of the table.

"You don't have to go if you don't want to." It was all he could manage.

Her eyes seemed to bore into him through the smoke. "You want me to stick around?" The night seemed to have broken her out of her apathetic state.

Spider sipped his drink. "Maybe." He felt like an idiot. God was right. If he felt something, he should just tell her. But did he? Was it just pity or compassion that made him feel this way? He had never been in touch with his emotions, at least on a level that allowed him to analyze them to any degree. But now? Something was different. Maybe it was the death of Takashi that had brought this on. Even as that thought rolled through his head, he knew it was a lie, a rationalization. He had felt something the minute she had turned those eyes to him, and he knew it. Was God right?

Kimber rolled the ash off her cigarette in the ashtray. "So say it."

Spider wanted to, he could feel it now, but what would happen if he did? He had a team to run, he had business to do, money to make. How would this—

Before the train of thought could continue, his smartphone trilled within his jacket. He slid the phone out, knowing what the call was about. "Yeah?"

It was Thrash. "Smith is here. He's driving a black Halperin Ghost. Meridian spotted him outside and knocked on his window. She just relayed the message. He doesn't get out of the car, apparently. I guess you should send her out."

"I'll take care of it." He hung up and pocketed the phone. "Tosh, come with me. Smith is outside." He stood up and offered Kimber his hand. "Time to go."

Kimber stared at him for several seconds, then crushed her cigarette out in the ashtray and stood up. She did not take his hand. Instead, she waited for him to walk ahead of her, while Satoshi brought up the rear, her eyes scanning the area as she moved. The club was nowhere near as busy as it was earlier in the night, but since it never closed, there would be people in and out until around nine or ten tonight. Then the nightly regulars and new customers would stream in, and it would start all over again.

Down the stairs to the first floor, where drunks and info-junkies and addicts and other citizens sat at tables alone or in small groups. Spider led the way through the rabble to the lobby, where Faith the Greeter-Bot told them to have a nice night. He held the door open for Kimber, but she said nothing as she walked past him.

Outside, the rain continued to fall, heavier now. Spider thought absently that it would continue into the so-called "daylight" hours. Since the Red was in a direct path from Orange District, the city's unregulated industrial sector, daylight was nearly non-existent here because of the air pollution. The same group of Harajuku Girls that he had seen down the block were hanging around on the corner, laughing and talking and acting as if it wasn't three-forty-five in the morning. Across the street, he could see a group of hackers tapping into a land-line for nefarious purposes. He could smell noodles and fish from the market down the block.

The Halperin Ghost was parked directly in front of the club, its engine still running. Spider could see a man in a dark jacket behind the wheel and assumed this was Smith. He stepped forward and opened the Ghost's passenger door. Kimber slipped past him and moved towards the car. He watched her duck her head as she climbed into the seat. She looked up at him one last time.

Spider ducked down and glared at the man behind the wheel. "You're Smith?"

"I am," came the terse reply.

"Keep her safe," was all he could manage before Kimber pulled the door shut. She turned her eyes away from him, then met his gaze once more as he stepped away from the car. The Ghost revved its engine, then pulled away from the curb. Kimber was still looking at him as the car drove away.

Spider pulled his phone from his jacket and punched in a number. Severen answered after the first ring. "Yeah?"

"You got the car?"

"I got it, boss."

"Good. Follow it all the way there. If something happens, let me know. When she gets there, stay with her and call me. Then set up a secure connection to the Green District cameras outside that building."

"You want fries with that, boss?"

"Don't be a smart ass. And find me God. I want to talk to her."

"Got it, boss."

Spider hung up the phone and dropped it into his jacket pocket. He turned to the door, but Satoshi was already there, holding it open. The rain slid down his neck, getting under his suit. He could feel it gliding down his back. He headed for the door.

"Everything alright, Spider?" Satoshi asked him as he passed her, moving into the club's lobby.

"Not anymore, Satoshi."

"Can you at least tell me what exactly is going on?" She followed, letting the door close behind her.

~~~

Kimber tried not to look at the man next to her, the man named Smith. He did not speak to her as she got into the car, nor did he speak as he raced away from the club, weaving through traffic like a mad man. Cabs and pedestrians zipped by her window, but the man did not slow down. At a red light, the man honked his horn and blew straight through, barely slowing.

She tried to focus on the sights outside the window, the things she had heard so much about before coming to this part of the city. Now, she thought, she would probably never set foot here again. She had no reason to. The implant was out of her body, the bullet wound was cleaned and sewn up, and … and …

Kimber's face turned dark. She wouldn't think of him. She wouldn't.

The car drove through another intersection. Again, Smith didn't stop. He stared straight ahead and kept both hands on the wheel, ten and two. The silence was killing her. She needed the noise to drown out the sounds of her own mind, the things she didn't want to think about right now. Like him. Kimber squeezed her eyes shut, trying to kill the thoughts. But they wouldn't leave. He was everywhere.

But why? He was no one to her. He was doing his job, nothing more. The Cyber Princess had told her that he would be abrasive, cold. But he was not. He had shown her more compassion than her own friends and family. He, and his team, had kept her alive. They had delivered her to a Surgeon who had removed her implant, exactly what they said they would do. Exactly what the Cyber Princess had told her would happen.

So why did she have these feelings?

She tried to focus on what her new life would be like. Would she meet others like herself, people who had the same … problem that she did? Would they be accepting of her? It was a reasonable question. She had not seen much acceptance in the three years since her ordeal began, the day after her twenty-fifth birthday. Where would she live? What kind of job could she hope to find with a year-long gap in her employment history?

Outside the window, the city passed by her, just people living their lives with no idea what lay ahead of them. Just like her. She wondered if some of these people had been through what she had. Not just tonight, but for the last three years. Did they know? Had they seen what she had, felt the sting of the needles? If so, would she meet them soon?

Her life had been solitary for the last year or so. Friends had gradually given up on her. Same with her family. They all thought she was nuts, that the stories she told were just that. No truth needed to be attached to her statements, since they came from the mouth of a crazy person.

She wondered if the same thing was happening to the people outside the window.

Smith made a left turn despite several honks and kept driving. His face was blank, as if he were asleep. Kimber wondered how often he did this, ferrying people to their destinations like some sort of high-priced limo service. Because she had no doubt that a man who was referred to as a "transporter" was highly paid for his services. Otherwise he would be nothing more than a chauffeur.

She turned away from him and faced the window once more, giving up on trying to read his face or see something in his eyes. He didn't want her to, simple as that. Probably a defense mechanism. This man Smith would feel no guilt or sadness if she died, since he knew nothing about her and didn't want to. Kimber felt a sense of profound pity for the man. Did he have someone, or something, to care about? Was this what she would become, down the road?

She made a promise to herself that she would find something, or someone, to care about. She would not let herself become a shell, an empty vessel. Even if what she had gone through did not stop the abductions, and she had been told that it might not, she still wouldn't let herself become cold, empty. Down that path lay hopelessness. She could not afford that, not now.

A right turn, and Smith was barreling down a road that would lead him straight into the Green District, she knew. While she did not call Millennium City home, she was familiar with the layout, just like everyone else in the country. The city was a hub, a mecca. It was pre-mil New

York and Los Angeles rolled into one, or so she had been told. She had been only a year old at mil-turn.

She could feel pangs of hunger growing in her stomach. She wondered if this man Rechter knew where to find something to eat at this hour. The idea brought other thoughts into her head. How would she find a place to live? How could she simply be expected to start over at twenty-eight? She had worked to build a life and now … it was just gone. Over. She had nothing but the clothes on her back.

It was all she could do to hold back the tears that threatened to spill over, that she had been holding back for so long now. But she wouldn't cry. Not in front of this man Smith, who she didn't even know. If she needed to do it so badly, she could wait until she got where she was going for the night. Somewhere safe. Then she could let it out, if she still needed to.

The car rode on for another thirty minutes, by her count, and she was left with only her thoughts.

The Halperin Ghost made a slow right turn, then accelerated down a nearly empty street. The Green District did not have the reputation of the Red, and so it was less populated at this time of the night. The car passed through three intersections before it pulled over to the curb and came to a stop.

Smith turned and looked at her. "This is your stop," he said, his voice flat.

Kimber opened the door and got out of the car. When the door shut, the Ghost pulled away and drove off, leaving her standing on the curb.

She looked up at the building in front of her. It was small compared to what she had seen tonight, only twelve stories. The steel door was set into the front of the building just after a set of stairs. As she climbed to the door, it swung open and a man stepped out.

There was a softness to his face that Kimber had not expected. He was clean-shaven, also unexpected, and he had spiky dark hair that had been shaved down on either side, giving him a punkish look that Kimber found comforting. He wore a hooded sweatshirt with Savage Dragon on the front and an old pair of blue jeans. As he caught sight of her, he smiled. "Are you Jennifer?"

Thomas Rechter

Kimber nodded and said, "Yes." She supposed that, after all this, she *was* Jennifer now. Kimber would be left behind, a remnant of her old life.

"I'm Rechter. Come on in," the man said. He stepped aside and let her pass.

The interior of the building was surprisingly warm, shocking her out of her state. She turned to this new man as he closed the door behind her. A set of keys jingled in his hand as he led the way down a hall to a set of stairs. "I'll show you where you'll be staying."

Kimber followed him up several flights to the seventh floor. Here, he swung a stairwell door open and led her to another hallway, this one painted white and lined with doors. "Not many of these are occupied right now," Rechter said. "If your unit isn't up to par for whatever reason, let me know and we'll get you moved."

Kimber nodded, but did not speak.

"Rent is six-fifty a month. Cheap for this part of town, but not as cheap as the Red. It's not much, but it'll give you something to work for. Utilities are included in that, by the way. And if you—"

Kimber stopped listening for a moment. Rent? What was this about? "I'm sorry," she began, "but I don't think I understand. What do you mean, rent?"

Rechter stopped and turned his eyes to her. "They didn't tell you?"

"Tell me what?"

Rechter tried to smile at her. He seemed to have trouble with the gesture. "This isn't a one-night thing, Jennifer." He swept a hand behind him. "This is your home. Everybody that lives here? They're just like you. Well, with one future exception. He'll be moving in here in a week. But that's it."

"What do you—"

"This isn't any apartment building. I assume whoever got you here told you who I am and what I do."

"Not exactly."

"Well, you could call this a halfway house for abductees like yourself. Most of them have had their implants removed and their lives are returning to normal, slowly but surely. The difference is, I don't kick you out at any time for any reason. We're a community here." He began to walk once more. "I'm not supposed to know where you came from, understand? I don't mean your hometown, I mean who got you here. We keep it all separated, that way no one person knows everything. Helps keep us and you safe." He stopped outside of a door and used a key from his ring to open it. "This is your apartment for as long as you want it to be. You're month to month with this place. If you feel you want to leave, you are free to do so. I don't keep records so there's no paperwork to sign. And if you want your name to be Jennifer, then that's what it is."

To hear him use the name like it would be her own from now on triggered something inside her. She couldn't run from it, couldn't hide from it. Her past belonged to her, and no one else. She had to own it, had to make her peace with it eventually. Running didn't solve anything. For the second time tonight, she whispered, "My name is Kimber. Kimber Kane."

She watched the smile on his face as it grew. "My name's Thomas Rechter." He shook her hand gently. "Nice to meet you, Kimber Kane." The key ring went into his left pants pocket. From the right pocket, he withdrew a smaller set of keys and dropped them into Kimber's hand. "These are yours. There's sheets on the bed and towels in the bathroom." He hissed. "Almost forgot." A plastic card appeared in his right hand. He passed it to her. "This is yours. Get yourself some clothes, buy yourself some food, use it however you need to."

Kimber looked down at the piece of plastic. It was a gift card for Edge-Mart in the amount of nine hundred dollars. The number flashed at her in green neon from the card's left corner. "What ..." she stammered, but Rechter held up a hand.

"It's not charity and it's not a loan. I told you, use it how you need to. That should hold you over until you can get a job. Tomorrow, when you feel up to it, go down to the fifth floor and knock on 5D. Tell Eric that I sent you when he answers, because he always does. His wife Marion was talking about some openings at the noodle house where she works, over in Yellow District. It's not much, but it'll get you started."

Kimber was beyond shocked. "How do you ... how does ... who pays for all of this?"

"I do," Rechter answered, not missing a beat. "Try to get some sleep. And don't worry. You're safe here."

"Thank you," she managed, holding back a sob of gratitude. No one had ever been this nice to her, least of all a stranger she had just met. Her own family hadn't done this for her.

"You're welcome. Rest. You'll feel better in the morning." He pointed to her arm. "Doctor Crohm lives in 10F. Go see him tomorrow and he'll change those bandages for you." Rechter turned and began to walk down the hall.

Kimber stared after him for several moments, her mouth hanging open. How was all of this possible? How did—

"Stop worrying and go to bed," Rechter called over his shoulder. "Your life restarts tomorrow, Kimber." Then he pushed open the stairwell door and was gone.

Kimber stared at the keys in her hand and the apartment laid out before her. She could see that it wasn't large, but since she didn't have anything to bring into it, that wouldn't be a problem. It was enough. Maybe not forever, but who knew? Maybe she could make a life here. The hopelessness she had felt creeping into her mind earlier vanished. She could survive. More than that, she could become a person once more. She could get her life back.

~~~

Spider watched the Ghost drop Kimber at the curb on the large screen above his head. He watched her walk cautiously up the stairs to the door, watched the door swing open. He watched Rechter welcome Kimber into the building as if she were an old friend. He watched the doors close behind them. He watched it all from four different angles and a satellite.

As the doors on the screen closed, Spider folded his arms and turned his eye to the smaller screen on his right. "Happy now?" God asked on the screen. "She made it safe and sound."

Spider spoke into the headset he had slipped on thirty minutes earlier. "Thanks, Cyber. I owe you one."

The super-hacker smiled at him. "It was worth it to watch your heart grow three sizes like the Grinch on Christmas."

Spider shook his head. "You'll keep an eye on her?"

"I always do." She tucked a strand of red hair behind one ear. "I can see it on your face, Spider. You should've said something to her."

"Should've, would've, could've. Better off anyway."

"Bullshit. You're pissed at yourself and you know it."

Spider cast a quick glance over his shoulder at the tech monkeys, who were suddenly very busy with their consoles. Neither Thrash nor Severen would meet his eye. "I'm a thief and a felon. My life is here, in the Red, for better or worse. She doesn't need me fucking things up for her while she tries to rebuild herself and her own life. She's better off."

The super-hacker shook her head. "One of these days you'll quit lying to yourself, Spider. You're a human being, just like the rest of us."

"Doesn't pay the bills, sweetheart."

"Don't call me that." She looked away from the screen for a moment, then back to him. "I've got work to do here. Get some sleep, Spider. You look like you could use it." The transmission ended.

Spider took the headset off and tossed it to Thrash. "That's it, tech monkeys. I'm calling it. Go get some rest."

Thrash leaned back in her chair and stretched; Severen suppressed a yawn. "You sure, boss?" he asked. "We're not even tired—"

"Go. Hopefully we'll have another job tomorrow, but for now, go back there—" He pointed to the living quarters. "—and get some sleep. I'm going to have a drink." He looked at Thrash. "Then I'm going to call Finnegan myself and get Tak brought back here, okay? Don't argue with me, just go back there and get some rest. You've been awake for almost twenty-six hours at this point. Go."

Thrash glared at him but said nothing. The bags beneath her eyes said it all. She stood up and moved past him into the living quarters, heading for her own cot.

Severen stood up as well. "I'm going to find Dauphine."

Spider chuckled. "Good luck." He began to head for the door. Before he reached the spiral staircase, his phone rang. This stopped Thrash and Severen in their tracks. Spider dug the phone out of his jacket and answered. "Yeah?"

He heard the familiar hisses and static, indicating a secure connection was being made. There was a second of hesitation after the hissing stopped, then a female voice asked, "Is this Spider?"

"Yes. Who is this?"

"My name is Allegra Flynn. I understand you stole something of mine tonight?"

Spider felt a strange grin spread across his face. "I did. But let's be clear, Miss Flynn: you tried to steal something of mine as well. And your goon squad killed my friend. Now what exactly can I do for you?" The grin stretched wider. He couldn't help himself. "And make it snappy, sweet pants, because I don't have all night. Business, you know?"

She seemed to ignore his insult, but when she spoke again, Spider could detect a hint of anger in her voice. "It takes both brains and balls to hack my network. I appreciate both. I'd like to hire you."

"As what, a security consultant or something? Sorry, lady, but I don't work for the big corps."

"Not a salaried position. Off the books. You understand." She spoke a number that Spider was very familiar with. "That is your usual fee for a job of this type, correct?"

"Sure is."

"I'll triple it. For one night's work."

"That's a lot of money, but I don't think so. I read the papers and the news sites. I know what kind of business you do."

"Well, Edward Wallace Gibson, I suppose I can always make a call to the FBI. I'm sure they'd be very interested in your current whereabouts."

That was all he needed to hear. "Alright, I'm listening."

"I need you to steal something for me." There was another moment or two of silence. "It is now four-fifty in the morning here. At eight o'clock on the dot, data will be uploaded to the Kobiyashi corporate mainframe in Tokyo. The company, as I'm sure you're aware, has some of the best programmers in the world working for them. Their network is more secure than some governments. The data, well … you stole it once tonight. I have every confidence you can steal it back. Does that sound like something you can handle?"

Spider snapped his fingers and indicated the tech monkeys' consoles. Thrash and Severen were back in their seats in seconds, slipping their headsets back on. "Yes. For triple the money and not a penny less."

"Excellent. Now—"

"But know this: you have just made an enemy of me. That is not a statement that I make lightly, do you understand?"

The voice laughed, and Spider felt his face flushing red. "I am not afraid of you, Mister Gibson. Do your worst."

Spider listened as the woman laid out the job for him. Easy pickens, it seemed. He briefed his team after he got off the call, then instructed Thrash to find God for him. It took five minutes.

Her hair was still pulled back, but she was wearing a different shirt and had make-up on. "What is it, Spider? I told you I was busy."

"I just got blackmailed into a job. I need your help with this one."

Now he had God's attention. "Tell me."

Spider ran her through it in less than a minute, then folded his arms. "What do you think?"

God grinned at him. "I think I'm going to have a lot of fun today, Spider. Thanks for that. Not that I needed another reason to fuck over Flynn International after what happened tonight."

"So what will it take for you to crash the Flynn corporate servers at this time of the morning?"

God shook her head. "Nothing. Give me ten minutes. You owe me now, Spider, got it? This is big time. Flynn International doesn't play by the rules."

"I'm aware of that. Hence the reason why I called you. Fight fire with fire."

The super-hacker smiled at him. "Aw, Spider, you flatter me so. I'll call you back in ten." The transmission switched off.

Spider stepped outside for a smoke while he waited, knowing full well that it would not take God ten minutes to do anything. She could make tea faster than that, he imagined. No, he would get the call much sooner. Then he could get started.

He was fully aware of the risk involved in what he had planned. Breaking into Kobiyashi was something his people could do in their sleep, especially with God backing them up. That wasn't the risk. It was in what he planned to do with the data once he got ahold of it. Running a play on Flynn International, and on Allegra Flynn herself, was known throughout his business as "the death card". You played it only when you wanted to die, because that was exactly what they would do to you, and not in a quick and pretty way. Allegra Flynn was not someone to be trifled with, and he knew that. But after tonight, he wasn't sure if he particularly cared anymore.

He pitched the butt off the catwalk and into the alley below him. The alley was empty, because the girls were in the middle of a shift change right now. Quartez insisted on twelve-hour rotations. It was hell on the girls, but it was a boon for their bank accounts. Spider swung the door open after entering his code and went downstairs.

God called back a few minutes later. "It's done. Get into Kobiyashi and get the data. After that, you've got ten minutes. The virus is set to go off exactly at eight-ten, understand?"

"And?" Spider asked.

"And it'll cripple their network for a few hours, maybe a day at the most. Not that it'll do much good. Flynn has servers all over the world and I can't crash them all. You're basically slapping her across the face."

"That's the idea. Nobody calls me up and blackmails me into a job."

God smiled at him and chuckled. "Allegra Flynn isn't just anybody, Spider."

He smiled. He had just been thinking the same thing. "And neither are you. That's why I called."

"Do the job, Spider. But … you want some advice?"

"Doesn't mean I'll take it, but sure."

God's face became serious in a way that Spider had rarely seen before. Her eyes were like orbs of fire. "Destroy it. Whatever it is. Don't even look at it first, just kill it. If she wants it back so bad, destroying whatever it is will do more damage than I can from here."

"I'll take it under advisement."

"With you, that usually means no. I'm serious, Spider. Destroy it."

"Yes, mother. Anything else?"

"Yeah. Watch your back. If Flynn already knows you stole from her two or three hours after you pulled the job, then I'd say it's a fair guess that she's got a hard-on for you. Why, I couldn't guess. But if she's calling you like this, you're on her radar in a big way. And that isn't good."

"Understood." He grinned. "You're forgetting one thing, though. This is my city. She wouldn't dare try it here."

"Don't be so sure."

"One more thing. Can you keep an eye on the place for a few hours? I've got something I need to do."

God gave him a look. "As if I didn't know."

"You're too smart for your own good."

"You're not the first person to tell me that. I'll make sure the place doesn't burn down, Dad. Watch your back."

"I'm over and out, God."

"Take care of yourself, Spider." She ended the transmission.

Spider tossed his headset onto Thrash's desk. "Get everything ready," he said.

"On it, boss," Severen replied.

"Let's get this done." Spider sat down on the ratty sofa and took a deep breath. He could feel the weariness in his bones, the signs of his body telling him that he needed to sleep. But he couldn't, not now. There was business to be done. He didn't give a shit about the money. This was about making an example of Allegra Flynn. He personally did not care how powerful the woman was. All of that counted for very little here in the Red. She could be killed on the street just as easily as anyone else could. More so, if she was clustered in the center of a group of bodyguards. One shot from a roof top and it was done.

But he didn't want that. He wanted to show everyone, in the Red and out, that he was not to be fucked with. Even by someone as perceivably powerful as Allegra Flynn.

He took another deep breath, then stood up. "How's it going?"

"We're on our way," answered Thrash. "Should we get in and camp out?"

"Yeah." He checked his watch. "You've got a little under three hours." Then he turned and headed for the stairs. "I'm going to … run an errand. I'll be back in two hours or so. Go to work." As he began to climb the stairs, he could see the tech monkeys working their consoles, tapping keys. The image made him smile. *Bring it on, Miss Flynn*, he thought.

~~~

The black Halperin Farmiga pulled out of the VASU into the rain, turning right and heading down Desperation Avenue. The car's horn honked several times to clear pedestrians from in front of it, oblivious to the stares and middle fingers it received.

Inside the car, Spider sat behind the wheel. Riding in the passenger seat next to him was the pulse-pistol he kept hidden beneath his table. The car's stereo was on, playing a tune that he didn't recognize, but felt strangely appropriate. The lyrics told of a search for the meaning, or the soul, of a man. Spider found he could relate.

The drive took him out of the Red and into Green District, leaving behind the glaring neon and the gangs and the polluted air. Here, as the sun began to rise on his right, he could actually smell and taste a difference. It grew more and more obvious as he drove further into the Green. He rolled down his window and let the air flow through the car. After a few minutes, he lit a cigarette.

The Farmiga's in-dash GPS guided him through the unfamiliar city district. He lived and worked in the Red. It was his comfort zone. As much as he despised the place, it was the best district in the city for his type of business. It was nearly impossible to get nailed by a police bust, because they never came into the Red, unless they were looking for a little action from some of the hookers. Here, in Green District, he had to admit that he was out of his element. But the more he thought about it, the more he realized that it was the best thing for her. She didn't need all the confusion and gray areas that came with life in the Red. She needed stability after what she had been through.

Spider made a right turn, following the robotic GPS voice's instructions. He pitched the cigarette butt out the window but didn't bother to roll it up. Instead, he rolled it down further and let the clean, or cleaner, air wash over him. It was a nice break from the foul muck that he breathed every day in the Red.

He reached the building much quicker than he thought he would. Before he knew it, he was pulling the Farmiga over to a designated parking space and searching his pockets for change to feed into the meter. When he realized he didn't have any, he used a fake credit card to cover the charge. He made sure the Farmiga was locked, then he climbed the building's imposing staircase to the front door.

Here, he found that his hand was trembling as he reached for the door handle. Was he doing the right thing? Did it make sense to just show up at her door like this? What if she didn't want to see him? He tried not to think about it as he pushed the front door open.

In the building's main corridor, he found himself staring at a wall filled with mailboxes, each marked off for a particular apartment. Mopping the floor next to these was a man wearing a Savage Dragon hoodie who looked to be around Spider's age, maybe a few years older. The man looked up as Spider approached him. "I'm wondering if you can help me," Spider said as he reached the man.

"That depends. What do you want?"

"I'm looking for Jennifer."

"No Jennifer here, buddy. Sorry." The man lifted his mop and continued his work.

Spider tried again. "How about Kimber Kane?"

Now the man stopped his mopping and looked up again. "Who are you?"

"I'm a friend."

"What kind of friend?"

"Is she here or not?"

The man looked Spider up and down for several moments, as if he was assessing him for some unknown purpose. Finally he said, "She's on the seventh floor. Apartment 7H. If anything happens to her—"

"Nothing will." Spider turned away from the man, who went back to his mopping, and walked until he found a stairwell. It did not stink of stale piss and staler alcohol like he was used to, and it wasn't filled with trash either. He made his way up to the seventh floor, noticing that not a speck of dirt or garbage was present anywhere. He wondered if the building's super used a service or if the janitor he had just seen was on his own.

Spider pushed the stairwell door open and found himself in another corridor, this one painted white and filled with doors. He counted off the apartments as he made his way down the hall, until he reached 7H. Spider took a moment to compose himself before he knocked on the door.

He could see the peephole in the door's center darken for a moment before the door swung open into the apartment. It was dark and smoky inside. Spider could smell imitation tobacco from within. Kimber stood in the opening, one hand on the door frame, her eyes locked onto his.

"I don't know what I'm doing here," Spider finally said, after he had stared at her for several moments.

"Yes you do." Kimber stepped aside. "Why don't you come in?"

"Are you sure? I can't … stay long and I—"

"Come in or don't."

Spider stepped over the threshold and Kimber closed the door behind him. He found himself in a small studio apartment. There was a double bed against the far wall on his right, and a small kitchen to his immediate left. In between, he could see a couch and coffee table, along with a small flat-screen television and keyboard for internet access. The walls were bare of artwork or posters, giving the place a mock-up feel, as if it wasn't real. Kimber glided past him into the tiny kitchen, not looking at him as she stepped up to the counter. "Want some coffee?"

"That sounds good." Spider cursed himself for his words. Why was he bothering to make small talk with her? What was the point? He knew why he had come here, that whole line at the door was nothing but a lie and he knew it. So why couldn't he just say that to her? He turned towards her, but found he was looking at her back as she loaded up a cheap Hadida coffee maker with what looked and smelled like Colombian. She switched the machine on and it emitted a burbling noise as it began to cycle.

Kimber turned around, leaning against the counter, and stared at him. She didn't speak, but she didn't need to. He could see it all in her eyes. *She* knew why he was here, even if he felt the need to lie about it. *That makes one of us*, he thought, mostly because he still wasn't sure exactly what he was doing here. As in, he knew why he had come, but he didn't know what he expected to happen now that he was here. It was a strange feeling for him. He wondered how Kimber felt about it.

"Are you going to say anything?" Kimber finally broke the silence.

Spider found it hard to speak. "I'm … not sure what to say."

The coffee maker spat and hissed behind her, then beeped twice to signal the end of its cycle. Kimber waited another moment for him to say something, then she turned around and began to pour the fresh coffee into cheap ceramic mugs that she pulled from a nearby cabinet. "How do you take it?" she asked without turning around.

"Black with sugar."

He could hear the clink of a spoon as Kimber stirred in what was no doubt artificial sweetener of some sort. Real sugar wasn't easy to come by anymore, and the fake stuff

CARTER JOHNSON

was a third of the price of the real thing. Kimber stirred the sweetener into her own cup, then lifted both mugs and turned around. She offered one to Spider, passing it over the counter to him. Now, she leaned against the counter with her mug in hand and stared at him as she took a sip. Spider brought his own mug to his lips and took a swig. The coffee was just right, the sweetener just so, and he could instantly feel his body perking up. He needed this more than he realized. He took another long sip, savoring the rich brew, then set his mug down on the counter. "You make a great cup of coffee," he remarked.

Kimber stared at him over the rim of her mug. "But you didn't come here for that, did you? So why are you here?"

Spider found that his mind was suddenly full of words, all the right ones he needed to express himself to her in just the right way. But they were jumbled like puzzle pieces still in a box, and he couldn't pick the right ones out of the bunch. He searched and searched, racking his brain, but the correct words would not rise from the pile. So he said fuck it. "This isn't something I normally do," he began, punctuating the sentence with another sip of coffee. "I'm not … I don't have many friends. Relationships are not my strong suit. I'm a criminal, and I make my living that way." His eyes softened as he set the coffee mug down. "You can't … there's no way for you to understand a lot of this. You and I … we come from opposite ends of the spectrum—"

"What makes you say that?" Kimber interrupted.

"Look at you," he blurted out. "You're beautiful and smart and you have your whole life ahead of you—"

"How young do you think I am? Because I'm actually twenty-eight."

Spider was mildly astonished. She certainly didn't look that age. In fact, she looked barely old enough to drink alcohol. But what did he know?

"And I don't have it all together. Look at what I've been through tonight, and that's only a fraction of the hell my life has become for the last three years. But now I can change that." She pushed off from the counter and made her way out of the kitchen. In seconds, she was standing in front of Spider, staring into his eyes. "I don't know where my life is going now, but I have a chance to make it better. And I'm going to take it." Neither one of them seemed to be adept at expressing their feelings tonight. Spider thought he could see a glimmer of it in the corner of her eye, but he wasn't going to speak first. Kimber dropped her eyes for a moment, then refocused on him. "There's a ... place for you in there, if you want it." She looked away again, and moved off to his left. "I'm not saying I'm going to be ... perfect. And I don't expect you to be, either. But ... this is a cold city. I learned that much tonight. I could use the warmth."

Spider ran a hand through his peroxide hair. "I'm not very good at warmth. I don't ... I haven't had a lot of use for warmth in my line of work."

"That's okay. I'm not very good with people anymore. Two years on my own."

Spider turned to face her. She was standing by the apartment's large window, holding her mug in one hand and staring out into Green District. "I don't want to hurt you."

"You won't." She turned. "I'm tougher than I look."

"That you are," Spider said, and managed a tiny smile.

~~~

CARTER JOHNSON

The Farmiga returned to the VASU at eight minutes after seven o'clock in the morning, gliding through the parking deck's entrance like a dark wraith. Spider used another fake ID card to park the machine, and waited until he reached the sidewalk before lighting another cigarette. He eyed the pack's interior. Only seven left. Kimber had put a dent in the pack, and he knew he would need to stop at Doom's Market later on today and get some more. This time, he told himself, he wouldn't settle for just the one pack. Even if Doom tried to talk him out of it, which wasn't uncommon.

The rain had slowed enough now to be only mildly annoying. Spider cupped his cigarette in one hand as he moved down the sidewalk, his eyes scanning the shops and restaurants around him. His stomach gave a lurch as he caught a whiff of sushi and noodles from one of the shops on his left. He hadn't eaten in several hours, and he knew that if he wasn't going to sleep anytime soon, he would have to recharge himself with food instead. He made a note to send one of the tech monkeys out for some breakfast when he got back to the Hive.

He slowed as he approached the news screens on Kilgore, wanting to get a shot of fresh news before he hit the Hive. But as he crept into the bustling activity, he found that the bottle-blond on the screen was still spouting off the same stories he had seen several hours ago. Even the scroll below her babbling face had not changed much. The only new story he could see was something about President Beckerstaff's motorcade hitting an IED during his "humanitarian" tour of Spain. Unfortunately for the country, Beckerstaff was very much alive and doing just fine, although two of his immediate staff had been killed in the blast. The news feed switched to a video of a somber

Beckerstaff at a podium, faking the tears he was trying to hold back as he described the deaths of his staff members. Spider turned away in disgust; the only thing Beckerstaff cared about was himself. As far as Spider was concerned, the man was an undiagnosed psychopath. It had been him who had gutted the Clean Air Act and de-regulated much of the country's business and industrial sectors. It was him who allowed the Red to be filled with polluted air every single day.

Spider moved on, trying to banish the image of Beckerstaff from his mind. He smoked his cigarette until it was finished, then flicked the butt into the street, watching it bounce off the corner panel of a JR Cab.

As he reached The Cat O' Nine Club, he could see a group of circuiters leaving the building, their hardware gleaming in the half-light the Red referred to as dawn. He watched them walk across the street and continue down Desperation Avenue. Then he was inside.

Faith the Bot greeted him as he came into the lobby. He waved her off and kept going. Just inside the club, he could see Quartez by the stage, speaking in whispers to a group of girls that he vaguely recognized. His business was mostly done at night, so the five AM to five PM shift of girls were the ones he was familiar with. Day-shift was an entirely different operation, with its own group leaders and followers.

He crossed the large main room to the staircase and took it to the second floor, where he found Satoshi waiting for him in a chair by his table. *Why not?* he asked himself, and sat down, holding his hand in the air. Marisol had gone home for the night, so his request for a bottle and glass was filled by Saturn, the day-shift bartender. As the blond set the bottle and glass on the table, Spider felt a pang as he thought about Bridgit. Nothing he could do about it now. Saturn swept away towards the bar as he reached for the bottle.

"Little early, isn't it?" Satoshi asked. Then she smiled. "Should I call you 'boss'?"

Spider shrugged as he poured Chivas into the glass. "If you want. Tak did, and the tech monkeys do it all the time. Doesn't bother me, if that's what you're asking."

Satoshi leaned back in the chair. "Don't you think it's a little early, boss?"

"Not at all. I've been awake for over twenty four hours now. And I just drank three cups of strong Colombian coffee." He tipped the glass to her. "Your health." Then he sipped the liquor within and set the glass down. "Much better."

"You do this type of thing a lot?"

"Which part? Drinking at seven-forty in the morning?"

"All of it." She sat up and leaned forward. "What exactly is it that you do, Spider?"

"How much time do you have?"

"My time is your time now, as long as you're paying me."

"Touché." Spider sipped his drink. "Well, since God vetted you and gave you the okay, I guess—"

"Who's God?"

Spider finished off the glass of liquor in one swallow. "Okay. Listen closely, because I'm only going to run you through this once." He grinned. "I'll field questions after, okay?" He refilled his glass and took a long swallow before he continued. "I am part of a secret underground network that funnels alien abductees to surgeons in order to get their implants removed. What the implants' true functions are or whether or not aliens put them there is anyone's guess. All we know for sure is that the abductee can be tracked with it as long as the implant remains active by these … aliens. Nine times out of ten, the abductions stop once the implant is removed. In addition to that, there is a secret government agency referred to in slang terms as Men in Black who work very hard to get to those abductees first and … disappear them. Also, every other government in the world, as well as every large private corporation like Flynn International, wants to get their hands on these implants. The advances in weapons and technology are limitless and they know that." He paused and took a sip of his drink. "God is who I work for in this endeavor. She funnels the abductees to me, and I move them down the line. She's a hacker with a penchant for being overly paranoid. You met her earlier. She was the tiny head on the screen."

Satoshi was silent for several seconds. She turned and signaled Saturn behind the bar for another glass. When it came, she poured a generous amount of Chivas into it and gulped the liquor down.

"I thought it was too early for you," Spider remarked.

Satoshi shook her head. "That was before you started talking."

Ten minutes later, Spider and a stunned Satoshi were inside the Hive, standing before the main screen. Thrash and Severen were busy behind their consoles. Spider checked his watch, then re-folded his arms. He was nervous, not that he would admit it to anyone. This wasn't your run-of-the-mill data theft. This was the big leagues. Not only was he robbing one of the largest corporations in the world, he was being paid to do it by one of the world's *other* largest corporations.

"Two minutes," Severen announced, not taking his eyes off the console screen in front of him. Spider glanced at Thrash, who hadn't spoken since he returned. She was also staring at her console screen. He turned away.

"I still don't believe it," Satoshi muttered next to him.

Spider shrugged. "It's true."

"It can't be."

"It is."

"One minute," said Severen.

Spider glanced at the smaller screen to his right, where God was busy behind a keyboard of her own. He hoped this would work. On the larger screen, a visual representation of Kobiyashi's massive mainframe loomed over him. Data zipped around here and there while glowing text floated across the screen. Spider was having a hard time making sense of it, but he knew his tech monkeys were in their respective zones.

"Twenty seconds."

Spider waited.

"Now," Severen said, finishing his countdown. Before the word was completely out of his mouth, his fingers were racing across the console. The Hive was suddenly filled with the click of keys. Thrash was busy at her own console, blasting through corporate firewalls and other security measures.

It took ninety seconds.

"Got it," Thrash muttered, her first word in what seemed like hours.

"Get out," Spider said, his voice hard.

More tapping from Severen, then the large screen went dark. "We're out," he said. "We got it."

Spider uncrossed his arms and moved away from the screen, stopping between the tech monkeys' consoles. He glanced down at Thrash. "Is it encrypted?"

She nodded, not meeting his eyes. "Yes. But nothing we—"

"Then do it."

"Spider!" God shouted from her tiny monitor. "I told you to destroy that shit! Don't even look at it!"

"I want to know, and so do you. You're just hiding it better than me." He ignored her continued warnings. "Load it up. Bust through the encryption."

"On it, boss."

God didn't stop. "Spider, this is only going to make things worse for—"

"I don't give a shit anymore. This has gone too far for my tastes. That bitch isn't going to call me up and blackmail me into a damn job. She wants her shit back, she can have it. But not before I know why my ass was put in the sling."

God let it go for the time being, remaining silent. Spider knew she was just biding her time. If she truly didn't want him looking at it, she had ways of preventing it. But he had a feeling she wouldn't do that, not now. She was just as curious as him.

Thrash tapped several keys and suddenly the large screen lit up with diagrams and scrolling text. There was more information on the screen in one single second than Spider could process. Not that it made much sense to him anyway, since he wasn't a tech guy. That's why he had a team. And not just any team, but the best.

"What am I looking at?" Spider asked, but he received no response. When he turned around to face his team, both Thrash and Severen were staring at the screen with open mouths. "Well? What is it?"

"A development file," Thrash finally said. Her eyes were the size of quarters. "For the implants. Everything that Flynn has done with the ones they've collected for the last ten years. Everything they've tried to adapt the technology to: missile defense, aerial combat, all of it."

"This was what she wanted back," Spider muttered to himself.

"Now you know," God said. Spider turned his gaze to her screen, and she met his eyes. "This is why they were after the girl tonight. Why everyone was. Do you see now?"

He did, but he didn't want to. God had mentioned that abductees were disappearing, and he knew from his own work in the field that abductions were becoming more and more common as the years went on. "So why did they want her?"

"Probably because that implant was adapted to her body. Maybe they don't know how to acclimate the implants to another body. Or maybe the implant is coded for a specific genetic profile, and it won't work otherwise. Who the hell knows, Spider?"

"You. You know. Or at least, you always act like you do." Spider was tired of this game. He wanted answers. "So tell me."

"You know what I know, Spider."

"Why don't I believe you?"

"Because you're paranoid."

"And you're not?"

God shook her head. "Beside the point."

"Which is?"

"Destroy the damn file, Spider. That's the only way you can un-fuck this situation—"

"I disagree. I think if I give her the file she wants, she'll back off."

"It's your funeral, Spider. But don't say I didn't warn you."

Spider shook his head and turned away, facing Thrash. "Copy this, then encrypt it and send it to God. She'll want to look at it."

"Spider—" God began, but was interrupted.

"I saw your face when it came up on the screen. You want it. Consider it a favor. Besides, I may need your copy for insurance."

"This is insane, Spider, you know that?"

"Trust me." He was about to tell Thrash to cut the transmission when his phone rang. He couldn't stop the smile that spread across his face. He knew who it was. Spider slid the phone out of his pocket and answered the call. "Miss Flynn. How nice of you to call at this hour."

The voice on the other end was full of ice. "Mister Gibson. I assume everything went as planned?"

"You assume correct."

"Excellent. Now, about the file?"

"I have it. Tell me where to send it. But I need to see the money first."

Allegra Flynn read off an account number, and Spider confirmed it was his. He snapped his fingers at Thrash, then rubbed his middle and index fingers against his thumb, a sign that he wanted Thrash to bring up his bank accounts. She complied, seeming to be out of her funk for the moment. The file's image disappeared from the large screen, replaced by numbered accounts in the Canary Islands.

"Ready when you are," Spider muttered into the phone. He watched the numbers shift on his main account, growing and growing until they stopped near the one-fifty mark. Spider felt his smile widen. Money had that effect on him.

"Satisfied?" Allegra Flynn asked, her icy voice seeming to mock him. She wouldn't think it was funny soon. He checked his watch. Two minutes.

"By you? Never happen." He couldn't resist. His natural reaction to authority was to buck it. "But the money helps."

"I would appreciate it if you saved the jokes for someone with a sense of humor, Mister Gibson. Now, my data?"

Spider snapped his fingers at Severen, who nodded and began the upload. "Sending it your way now."

"I can see that." Her voice remained flat and emotionless.

The upload was completed in another minute. When it was done, Spider said, "Now you have it. So back off, lady."

"I'm sorry, Mister Gibson. Did I give you the impression you had a choice in this matter, or any that may occur in the future?"

Spider chuckled. "Of course not. But I told you, I don't work for people like you. Check the file."

There were several moments of silence on the other end of the line, followed by whispers that Spider could not identify. This continued for several more seconds, until Allegra Flynn spoke once more. "This has been copied."

"That's correct."

"Mister Gibson, listen to me very carefully. That file—"

"Is now my personal property as well as yours. Nobody calls me up and blackmails me into a job. Not you. Not anybody."

"Then I believe a phone call to the FBI is in order. I won't be speaking to you again, Mister Gibson."

"The second you make that call, this file hits the web and every news site in the world. I will also personally e-mail copies to Kobiyashi Robotics and Galvatronix. Your biggest competitors will have every secret in that file."

"I can take the file back any time I want." Her anger was creeping into her voice. *Good*, Spider thought. He hoped he was getting under her skin.

"It's not here. Or anywhere that you'll ever find it. Come after me or try to fuck me into another job for you, I drop this on the world." He waited a few seconds for proper emphasis, then added, "It's not any fun when it's your own ass in the sling, is it?"

"If you read the news, you know what happens to people who threaten me or get in my way."

Spider shook his head. "You don't get it, do you? Ever heard of God?"

"The Christian deity? Of course I have—"

"No, not that God. The super-hacker. The one who cracked NORAD."

Silence on the other end. He couldn't help the smile on his face. "I'm familiar with her, yes."

"I bet. Legend has it that she was married to your brother years ago—"

"Never mention my brother again, Mister Gibson, or all the files in the world won't protect you from me. To respond to your statement: yes, she was married to my brother when he was still alive."

"Then you know who she is. The file is in her possession. Good luck tracking her down." He could hear a commotion from the other end of the line, and it made him smile as he checked his watch. The virus had gone off right on schedule. He hoped it ruined her perfect fucking day.

Allegra Flynn made a noise deep in her throat, a noise that Spider had never heard another human being make. It was a sound of pure anger. "You have made a very serious error, Mister Gibson. Unfortunately for you, this will not be our final conversation."

"Now it's my turn to say it: you don't scare me, lady."

"I will." The call ended.

Spider stared at his phone for a moment before he slid it back into his jacket. A deep breath, then he said, "That's it. All done for the night."

"This time you're serious, right?" Severen asked.

"Yes. Get some sleep."

The two techs backed away from their consoles and stood up. Thrash yawned and moved towards the living quarters, leaving Severen behind her. He looked as though he wanted to say something, but then thought better of it. He turned away and followed Thrash.

Satoshi, who had been nearly silent since she entered the Hive, was suddenly standing beside Spider. He hadn't even heard her move towards him. "I don't know about this," she said. "This is ... beyond me."

Spider was worried this might happen. "Not for you?"

She shrugged. "I'm sorry, Spider."

"Don't be. I just needed you for tonight. If this is something you're not comfortable with, that's fine."

"I just don't think ... you actually believe this shit?"

Spider grinned at her. "If you had spent the night in this room, you might believe it, too. But I understand what you mean. It's a lot to take in."

Another head shake. "I can't be a part of this, Spider. It's dangerous, and I have a family to take care of."

"I understand. Don't worry about it."

Satoshi touched him on the shoulder. "I can make a few recommendations, if you like."

"That would help. I'll need somebody pretty soon."

"I'll see what I can do."

~~~

Spider stepped out of the club and found that the rain had stopped and the clouds had moved on, leaving blue sky behind. Not that it mattered here. The Red was still gray and washed out from the air pollution. Spider watched a lone cyberpunk cross in front of him, eating noodles from a small carton. The sight made his stomach rumble.

He fished his cigarettes out of his jacket and lit one, staring up at the sky. Another day, and he still hadn't slept yet. *Fuck it*, he thought. He needed to eat. He had things to do. And he was planning on seeing Kimber later tonight.

A check of his watch revealed that it was half past eight in the morning now. He knew several places that were open right now, and not one of them was a bad place to eat. He took another drag of his cigarette and went right, making his way down Desperation Avenue towards Colton Street. There was a greasy spoon a few blocks down that always made him feel better when he'd had a rough night like tonight.

Another drag, and his phone rang. He wasn't surprised to see the number displayed. He slid a finger across the display and brought the phone to his ear. "Hey, Finnegan."

"Heard you needed me for something else."

"Yeah. Tak bought it on a job last night. He's a few blocks up from the club. Just need him brought back there."

"No problem."

"I'll meet you there in ten."

"Got it." The big man hung up.

Spider slid the phone back into his jacket, then swung around and reversed direction. He took a final drag from the cigarette and pitched the butt into the street. A JR Cab rolled over the butt and kept moving.

Spider ignored the sounds and smells of the Red around him, despite the rumbling in his belly. He could eat when this was done. For now, he had business to take care of.